THE MYSTERY ON SNAKE MOUNTAIN

A Jane Teaberry Mystery
Book 2

E. J. Garrett

* * *

ISBN 978-0-9991198-6-0

This book is dedicated to my daughters and granddaughters.

CHAPTER ONE
A TREASURE

"DOWN THIS WAY," said Jane, as she pointed towards the trail. She set her backpack on the ground and bent over to re-tie her hiking boots.

"I see it now," said her friend, Peaches. "This was a good idea to go hiking today. The weather is great! I hope I get some good pics."

"We were lucky since it's the weekend AND a nice day," said Jane. "After our first week of classes, I was ready to get outdoors and do just about anything."

"Me too," said Peaches, nodding in agreement. She hung her camera strap around her neck and lifted her small backpack over her shoulders to carry her water bottle and some snacks. Jane started down the hill on the trail, and Peaches started to follow her.

"Hey, slow down," said Peaches. "I'm still pulling it together here."

"Sorry," said Jane, slowing her pace to let

Peaches catch up.

Peaches tied back her curly black hair that she wore in long tight microbraids, and put on a brightly colored headband, while she walked along with Jane. "Keep in mind that I'm not an early morning person. I don't usually get up this early on a Saturday."

Jane smiled at her friend. She knew how much Peaches liked to sleep late whenever she had the opportunity. "I know. And I appreciate the effort. I promise it'll be fun."

Jane and Peaches had gotten an early start on the day, so the sun was just peeking over the horizon. The glow of the sunrise against the few puffy clouds was gorgeous. The rest of the sky was bright blue and the warm late August temperature was perfect for an early morning hike. Jane could smell the sweet honeysuckle bushes that lined the entrance to the trail. Birds were chirping out songs as they began waking up to the sunshine.

Eighteen-year-old Jane Teaberry had just started college in her hometown of West Midland at the local university. Jane and Peaches Parker, her close friend and doubles tennis partner from the high school tennis team, were now sharing a dorm room at school. They were both excited about this new chapter in their lives.

Peaches' dad, Dr. Parker, had been a Professor of Archaeology at the University of West Midland ever since their family moved to town from Florida last year. Peaches discovered that she loves small town life and wishes she had grown up here like Jane did. Peaches' mom is a medical doctor at the local hospital, so she is also called Dr. Parker.

Jane loved growing up in the small village of West Midland, just as her parents had. Nestled in trees in southwestern Ohio, the village has four beautiful parks, a college campus, a hospital, and a beautiful historic library. You can walk to the historic town square from just about anywhere in the village. Most residents who grew up in the village cherished their childhood years attending small town events with a tight-knit community.

The brush on the sides of the trail was thick with honeysuckle, nettles, and brambles, and there were large vines hanging from many of the trees. The girls could hear the hoot of a nearby owl, who had not yet gone to sleep for the day.

"It doesn't look like people venture off the path much," observed Jane, as they walked along. "Look at all the vines and stuff growing all over everything. I'm glad the trails are well-worn, so we know which way to go."

"I'll just follow your lead, since I've never been here before," said Peaches.

"I hope we don't find any snakes or poison ivy," said Jane. "I hate snakes."

"You'll know if I see a snake by the sound of screaming." Peaches laughed.

"Same here." Jane smiled.

"My dad said this is part of a historic serpent mound, where there was an American Indian village hundreds of years ago," said Peaches.

"Yes, this is the one, and I think there is a sign

somewhere near the other end that mentions it," said Jane. "I think it's a neat place to hike, but I haven't been here for a while. We used to hike here a lot when I was a kid. See how the earth is so much higher over there? That's part of the mound. We're at the tail end of it."

"Oh, yeah, I see it," said Peaches. "It looks like about six or seven feet higher along the side of the path. I think that people used to bury their dead in the mounds with some of their possessions and even some gifts to help them on their journey."

"That explains why they are so strict about people not being allowed to dig around here," said Jane.

The girls followed the trail down toward the river on one end and walked for a while before heading back up the hill on another path.

Jane stopped and pointed ahead towards the top of the hill. "We can follow the path by the mound along the bluff, and then it ends at a larger part, where I think is the center of the old village."

"Sounds good," said Peaches.

"People have found a lot of pottery, beads, and arrowheads over the years that they say is from the 1600s. I'm surprised your dad hasn't brought you here already, since he is an archaeologist," said Jane.

"I'm surprised, too, but we've only lived here a year, and it's been pretty busy," said Peaches. "I'm sure he'll get here soon, if he hasn't already. He's talked about it, though."

"There's also a large area just beyond the village

swimming pool where they found lots of bones. They think it was the cemetery for the village. Now it's just green space with a picnic shelter. You'll see it when we get that far. C'mon," said Jane, as she picked up her pace.

"I'm coming," said Peaches. "Just don't take off and leave me. We're supposed to be hiking together."

"Sorry," said Jane. "Check out this view from the top of the bluff." Jane charged ahead to the top of the hill, then stopped to stare out over the bluff into the sky.

"Nice," said Peaches, when she caught up. The sun had risen and there were billowy clouds that looked like balls of cotton. The rest of the sky was pure blue.

"I can see the river from here, and look at that morning sky. I think I can get some good pics." Peaches grabbed her camera and took several photos.

"Beautiful," nodded Jane, staring out over the river.

Peaches set her camera on a tree stump, and crept towards the edge of the bluff to look over. She stepped out onto a small flat ledge. "We're pretty high up from the river here," she said as she looked straight down the steep cliff.

"Be careful," said Jane. "It's a long drop from here."

"I will," said Peaches, holding onto some branches from a nearby bush. As she looked down, she spotted something sticking out of the side of the hill. "Look Jane, there's something down there. It might be an artifact – a old tool or weapon or something."

"I don't think there's room for me on that ledge," said Jane. "I'll stay back here and take your word for it."

"I'm going to climb down and get it," said Peaches. Before Jane could respond, Peaches took off her backpack and set it down on the ledge and started climbing down the side of the bluff backwards.

"It's not far," she called to Jane. "I'm almost there."

Jane could feel her heart pounding in her chest and could hardly speak. There wasn't anything she could do to stop Peaches from climbing down the bluff, and she was afraid she might fall. It was almost straight down to the river. Peaches had always been impulsive and Jane never knew what she might do at times.

Peaches stopped and held on with one hand while she grabbed the item and shoved it inside her sweatshirt to keep it safe. She grabbed a piece of rock that was jutted out above her to start climbing back up. Her foot slipped on the piece of rock below and she lost her balance. "Whoops!" she yelled.

Jane could feel her heart beating faster and her blood pressure rising. She gritted her teeth and held her breath. She was afraid to look down.

Peaches found a new spot for her foot, but it wasn't a good one, and she couldn't get back up.

"Jane, Jane, I'm stuck. Get some help!" she

called frantically.

Jane grabbed Peaches' backpack from the ledge and threw it behind her out of the way onto the trail. She stepped onto the small ledge and looked over at Peaches. She wasn't sure what to do, or how long Peaches could hang on if she called for help. She wasn't too far down, but far enough that Jane couldn't reach her. Jane looked around for something she could use to help Peaches. She spotted some large vines in a nearby tree.

"Hang on, Peaches," she yelled. Jane untangled the largest nearby vine and yanked on it to see if it was secure in the tree. She then hung it over the side of the bluff.

"Can you reach this?" she asked Peaches. It dangled just out of reach.

"No! I can't get it," called Peaches, hanging on with one hand and reaching out. Loose pebbles were falling from underneath her feet when she reached for the vine.

Jane held the vine and her breath and stepped back onto the small ledge. She pulled the dangling vine in closer until Peaches could finally reach it. She tried not to look at the river below.

"Got it," yelled Peaches.

"Let me know when you have a good grip on it and I'll try to pull you up." Jane was able to secure the vine around a large rock at the top.

"Ready," said Peaches.

Jane pulled on the vine and was able to pull Peaches up just enough to get a better foothold on the side of the bluff. Peaches grabbed a tree root sticking out of the dirt with her left hand. With her right arm looped around the vine, it gave Peaches just enough security to traverse her way back up to the top. When she reached the ledge, Jane grabbed her hand and pulled her back onto the surface of the ledge.

"Whew," said Peaches. "That was a little scary."

"No kidding," said Jane, with one hand on her chest, her heart beating wildly. "You almost gave me a heart attack."

"Sorry," said Peaches. "It looked easier than it was."

Jane took a few deep breaths of relief. Both girls sat down cross-legged on the trail away from the ledge and pulled out some water and snacks, while they calmed themselves down. Neither of them said anything for a bit.

Peaches suddenly remembered and pulled out the piece from her sweatshirt. "Look at what I found, though," she said. "Dad will love it!"

The item was about a foot long, wrapped in leather and colorful beads, with some feathers at one end. It was covered in dirt. Peaches lightly brushed off some of the dirt.

"Wow," said Jane. "It's pretty cool. I don't know how in the world you spotted it from up here. The feathers are a bit worn out, but the rest of it looks pretty good. I wonder what in the world it is."

"I guess I'm used to seeing all those artifacts that the Archaeology Department collects, so it just stood out to me," said Peaches. "It was just stuck there in the side of the hill and I could see the color of the beads and some feathers. It must have worked its way out over the years of weather and erosion. I can't wait to show it to Dad."

"I'm sure he'll be excited about it. But don't mention it to anyone else first, because I don't know if you'll get in trouble for taking it."

"I wasn't digging though. It was going to fall into the river soon," said Peaches.

"I know," said Jane. "But I just think you shouldn't say anything until you show your dad. He'll know the rules."

"Makes sense," said Peaches, nodding in agreement.

"Did you want to keep hiking, or are you ready to go?" asked Jane.

"I think I'm good for today," said Peaches. She smiled at Jane, who was relieved at her answer.

The girls headed back down the trail the way they came. Jane heard footsteps behind them on the trail, but each time she looked back, there was no one there. "Do you hear someone behind us?" she asked.

"Hmm," said Peaches, looking around. "I don't see anyone."

"I don't either, but I hear someone and I feel like someone is right behind us."

"I don't know." Peaches shrugged her shoulders. "Maybe it's the spirit of someone who lived here," said Peaches. "Maybe he's mad that I'm taking this artifact, whatever this thing is."

"Maybe," said Jane. "At least that would explain it."

They finally reached the edge of the woods. Jane was comforted to get Peaches away from the bluff, and breathed a sigh of relief. Peaches tucked the artifact back inside her sweatshirt so that no one else would see it before she showed it to her father.

The two girls started walking down the sidewalk toward the university. "I love living in a small town," said Peaches, as they walked back to the university campus. "Everything is right here and we can walk everywhere."

"I agree," said Jane. "I sometimes drive to get to my grandparents' house, though, just because it's faster, but everything in town is close by."

Jane had been living with her grandparents in West Midland for her senior year of high school, after her dad was transferred to Virginia to work for the FBI. Her mom died when Jane was just six years old, and Jane became close to her grandparents over the years, especially since they retired from the Army and had more free time to spend with her.

Jane's cousin, Ashley Fink, and her Labrador Retriever, Edward, lived in West Midland with Ashley's parents, ever since she returned from college in the Spring. She stayed with Jane at her grandparents' house for a while in the summer while they solved a few mysteries together.

Jane and Peaches returned to their dorm room. They were still putting things in place, as it was just the first week of school. They had set up their beds like bunk beds, with Jane on the top bunk and Peaches on the bottom. The room was small, but they had enough room for a desk, small dressers, two comfy chairs, a small refrigerator and a small TV.

"Home sweet home," said Peaches. "I'm not used to it yet, but I will be soon."

"It's cozy," said Jane, looking around at their new digs. She smiled at the picture of her mom on her dresser. She couldn't live somewhere without bringing her mom's picture along. Somehow, she felt protected with it always on her dresser.

Peaches caught Jane's eye looking at the picture. "Is that your mom?" she asked.

"Yeah," said Jane.

"I bet you miss her," said Peaches.

"I sure do," said Jane.

"I can't imagine life without my mom," Peaches said quietly. "I mean, she works a lot, since she's a doctor, but I can always count on her."

"This necklace I'm wearing was my mom's," said Jane. She tugged on it to show it to Peaches. "I never take it off, so I feel like she's always with me as long as I wear it."

"She's always with you anyway, but I'm sure it feels more like it when you're wearing something that belonged to her. What is that, a coin?"

Jane nodded. "It looks like a really old coin, but I don't know anything else about it. There's also something engraved on the back, but I haven't found out what it means. My dad gave it to me on graduation day, so I haven't had it very long. He found it when he was unpacking boxes, when he moved to Virginia."

"Maybe my dad would know what it says," said Peaches. "He speaks a few languages, since he's an archaeologist."

"Good idea," said Jane. "I'll have to remember to ask him."

Peaches pulled the artifact out of her sweatshirt and wrapped it up in another shirt and set it on the desk. "I'll just leave this here until we can take it to the Archaeology lab." She plopped down in a comfy chair and started taking off her hiking boots.

"Ick, look at all this mud on my boots. I'll set them over here by the door until I can take them into the laundry room and clean them off," said Peaches.

"Sounds smart. I'll do that, too," said Jane, as she started taking off her boots. "So, what is there to do around here when we're not in class?"

"I don't know," said Peaches. "I was going to go to the campus café this week to see what activities and clubs they have. They're supposed to have tables set up all week giving out information."

"Oh, good," said Jane. "I went to the ones at orientation, but they'll probably have more now. Let me know when you go and I'll come with you."

"Okay," said Peaches. "I'll probably go Tuesday. I just have morning classes, so I'll go after that."

"That works," said Jane. "Did you ever decide to join the tennis team? I didn't join yet, because I couldn't make up my mind. I think maybe I don't really want to commit to it. When does practice start?"

asked Jane.

"No, I didn't join, either," said Peaches. "I decided to see what else there is this year, but still want to play some tennis as much as possible. Hopefully we'll be able to use the university courts for some fun tennis."

"That's how I feel about it, too," said Jane. "There are so many options now that we're in college. I want to see what else is here."

Jane pulled out a plastic container from her dresser drawer. "My grandma sent us some brownies. Do you want one?"

"Are you kidding me?" said Peaches with a smile. "Hand 'em over."

CHAPTER TWO
A VISIT TO THE LAB

THE NEXT MORNING was Sunday and there were no classes. "Will your dad be in the lab today?" asked Jane.

"Possibly," said Peaches. "Sundays are an opportunity to catch up on things, so he often goes in and works after church. Mom has to work a lot of Sundays at the hospital."

The girls got some breakfast at the campus café before heading over to the Arts and Sciences Building with the wrapped artifact. Walking across the campus quad, they spotted Brandi Brown, who used to be the captain of their high school tennis team and used to bully Jane relentlessly.

"Oops, there's Brandi," said Peaches. "Should we turn this way and avoid her?"

"No, it's fine," said Jane. "She doesn't bother me anymore."

"Really? Well good," said Peaches, with a

surprised look.

Brandi spotted them and ran over. "Hi girls! So good to see you. What's that?" she said as she pointed to the wrapped artifact.

"Nothing important," said Peaches.

"Oh," said Brandi. "I thought you would be on the tennis team here, but I didn't see you at practice yesterday."

"No," said Jane. "I decided not to join this year. Sorry."

"Same here," said Peaches. "Maybe next year." Brandi had never bullied Peaches in high school, and she never was mean to Jane in front of Peaches. Jane wondered sometimes if it was because Peaches appeared so much more confident than she did.

"Well, that's too bad," said Brandi, looking uncomfortable. "If you change your mind, it might not be too late to join. I don't know anyone else on the team, and it would have been nice to have you two on it."

"We'll let you know if we do," said Jane. "See ya, Brandi," she said abruptly, as she kept walking.

"Bye, Brandi," said Peaches, as she followed Jane.

Peaches started laughing as soon as Brandi was out of earshot. "Who was that? Why is she being nice all of a sudden? She was like a different person."

"When I ran into her at orientation, it sounded like she had a reality check on what's important in her life. And yeah, it seems weird that she's being nice now. It's like she's somebody else, but I still know it's her," said Jane.

"I'm so glad she doesn't affect you anymore."

"Me too," said Jane. "It wouldn't make me feel better to be mean to her, just because she was so mean to me for so long, but I don't have to be her friend, either. I just want her to leave me alone."

"Yeah, I don't blame you for feeling that way."

"When I saw her at orientation, I realized I'm not afraid of her anymore. I think she bullied people because she felt like a weak person inside. I kind of feel sorry for her now."

"That's kind of interesting," said Peaches. "Feeling sorry for her after she was so mean to you." Jane just shrugged her shoulders.

They soon approached the Arts and Sciences Building and went inside. "My dad's office is on the second floor," said Peaches, as she pushed the elevator button.

The elevator doors opened on the second floor. "It's down this way," said Peaches. They reached Dr. Parker's office.

"It's not locked," said Peaches, as she tried the door knob. She opened it and they walked on in.

"Hi Dad," said Peaches with a smile. Dr. Parker got up from his desk and gave his daughter a big hug. When he stood up, Jane just now noticed how really tall he was. He was much taller than her dad, with short hair, dark skin and a mustache, wearing khaki pants and a light blue collared shirt, with an ID badge hanging from his shirt pocket. He wore a cool looking watch with all kinds of gizmos on it that Jane didn't recognize. She'd never seen anyone else with a watch like that. She guessed an archaeologist would need to know all sorts of things, so it made sense that his watch would have a lot of information.

"Hi sweetie," he said. "Such a nice surprise. I didn't know if you'd be visiting your dear old dad on campus."

"Of course," said Peaches. "You're still my dad. And now you work right near where I live."

Jane couldn't help being a little envious that Peaches' dad was right here on campus every day. She could go see him whenever she wanted. Jane's dad was only in town every few months and she didn't even get to talk to him on the phone very often. She missed him every day.

"Hi Jane. Nice to see you, too. What brings you two here this morning? Just a visit?" asked Dr. Parker.

"Well, yes," said Peaches. "But we brought something to show you that we found yesterday while we were hiking." Peaches unwrapped the artifact and handed it to her dad.

"Wow, this is a nice artifact," he said. "Wherever did you find it? You shouldn't be doing any digging around here."

"We weren't. I spotted it when we were looking at the river from the bluff by the mounds. It was sticking out from the dirt," defended Peaches.

"It was sticking out?" he asked.

"Yes, about three quarters of it was sticking right out of the ground on the side of the bluff. I could see some of the beads and feathers," said Peaches.

"Oh, I see what you mean. Erosion must have uncovered it," observed Dr. Parker.

"That's what I said," Peaches agreed.

"Well, this is a magnificent artifact. I'll clean it up and do some research, and then we'll have to turn it over to the West Midland Cultural Center museum in town. They've been displaying some of the local artifacts that were found from the old American Indian village."

"Great," said Peaches. "I couldn't just leave it there. It would have fallen into the river eventually and gotten lost forever." Peaches wasn't about to tell her dad about climbing down to get it and getting stuck and Jane having to rescue her with a vine.

"I knew you would know what to do with it," said Jane. Dr. Parker smiled at Jane and nodded. He handed Peaches back the shirt she had used to wrap the artifact.

"Let's take it in the lab and I'll put it in a safe place until I can clean it up," he said.

The girls followed him into the lab. "Would you like a tour while you're here?" he asked.

"Sure," Jane replied, before Peaches could answer. "That would be really cool."

"I'll put this piece in an empty drawer. Hang on a minute while I label it."

Jane and Peaches looked around the room while they waited. There were tables and chairs set up in clusters around the room. Two students wearing gloves were sitting at one of the tables working on some artifacts.

"This room is where the students work, cleaning and labeling artifacts from recent digs. Most students wouldn't be in here on a Sunday, but Chris and Kendra are grad students and they spend quite a bit of their free time here," said Dr. Parker.

Chris was dressed in denim overalls and a tank top, with his long brown hair pulled back in a blue bandana. He also had a short beard. Kendra had a short natural style hairdo and wore camo shorts and a pale yellow tee shirt that said "MY LIFE IS IN RUINS." They both looked up from their work and smiled and waved hello. Jane chuckled to herself when she read Kendra's shirt.

"These drawers and shelves across these walls contain artifacts that we brought back from digs. We put them in labeled drawers, and then when the students have time to work on them, they take items out and study them, measure them, take photos, and document them in our database. Then each item is placed in a plastic self-closing bag and labeled. Then they are stored in a different drawer with the other documented items from the dig in our storage room."

"Where was the last dig?" asked Jane.

"The dig was in the Southwestern U.S., in New Mexico. It was in Chupacabra County to be exact. A large privately owned estate that we believe was an American Indian village hundreds of years ago allowed us to investigate the area of the property where the village might have been."

"How many people went?" asked Jane.

"We had twelve students there for six weeks in

20

the summer. Most of the items have not been documented yet, so the students will have plenty to do this fall," said Dr. Parker.

"Wow, how interesting!" said Jane. "What kind of things did you find?"

Dr. Parker walked over to a drawer and opened it. "I think we found enough artifacts to declare that it was indeed a village at one time. We found a lot of items that were probably used for cooking, and some tools."

"Can we see some of them?" asked Jane.

"Here are a some of the things we found," said Dr. Parker.

He lifted up an item and held it out to show them. "A beveled flint knife. It was likely used for cutting wood. If you look closely, the bevel is on the left side. A right-handed person would pull the knife toward themselves when cutting wood."

He put the knife back and took out another item and held it for them to see. "Here is a larger blade that may have been a spear point. It would likely have been used for cutting up animals or for cutting out buckskin garments. These are the sorts of things we usually find. Tools, and toolmaking devices such as pieces of antlers, arrowheads, spears, pottery, etc."

Then he lifted up two rectangular items to show them. "These were unusual to find. These sand paintings were found right inside the opening of a small cave near where we were excavating. Sand paintings are used by the indigenous people in sacred healing ceremonies, but they are not made permanent

21

like these. They are normally very large in size. Sometimes they can be six feet long by six feet wide. They are always created on the ground and destroyed at the completion of the ceremony."

"That sounds very different than these. What kind of sand paintings are these?" asked Jane.

"Some tribes do make them for commercial sale, like a craft. However, some of the people were afraid that making a sand painting in any permanent form could cause evil things to happen to them. I am very curious why these would be hidden in a cave. They wouldn't be from a ceremony, and if they were made to sell, why would they be in a cave?"

"They look pretty old," noted Jane.

"It's possible they are old, but since they have been sitting in a cave, that could have sped up the aging process. We'll research them to find out who made them and why. I really don't know what to think about them."

"What's in the other rooms?" Jane asked.

"This smaller room over here contains an X-ray scanner to help us determine if there is something inside the item. And the room over here on the left is where we make molds of bones and other artifacts to recreate them for display in museums."

He walked into the molding room and Jane and Peaches followed. "That's why we have sinks and buckets and mold-making materials in here. This is just a different kind of work room."

Jane smiled as she looked around. "This is really neat. I might want to do this."

"We also have a room just for storage, where we keep the documented items arranged by dig site."

Just then a young man came out of the storage room. "This is Carl, my teaching assistant. He spends quite a bit of time here, too."

"Hi Carl," said Peaches. "This is my friend Jane." She turned to Jane. "Carl and I go way back. I've known him since Dad started working here."

"Hi Peaches," said Carl. "Nice to meet you, Jane. Sorry my hands are full," he said, as he carried a large tray of items over to one of the tables. "Are you an Archaeology student?" he asked, as he set down the tray.

"No, this is my first week of school and I haven't settled on a major yet. But I'm thinking I might want to study Archaeology. It looks really interesting from what I've seen so far," replied Jane.

"Great," said Carl. "I've tried to talk Peaches into it, but so far she doesn't seem interested."

"It's interesting, alright, but I don't know if it's what I want for a career," said Peaches.

"I understand," said Dr. Parker. "You need to find something you feel passionate about and that's alright with me if it isn't Archaeology."

"Well, Jane, if you have any questions about Archaeology or the program here, feel free to ask me anything," said Carl.

"Thanks, Carl. It was nice meeting you," said Jane.

Dr. Parker wrapped the sand paintings and put them back on the shelf, while Carl went back to work with the items on his tray.

"Dr. Parker, can I ask you a question?" said Jane.

"Well, of course," said Dr. Parker.

"When we were walking back in the woods by the mound, after Peaches found the artifact, I would swear someone was walking right behind us all the way out of the woods, but no one was there. I heard footsteps behind me the whole way. But whenever I looked behind me, there was no one. Are there ever any spirits or ghosts that stay in a place where people lived?" Jane asked. "I mean, would the people that lived in the village by the mound have an issue with items being dug up hundreds of years later?"

"Hmmm, well I will say some unexplained things have happened sometimes at digs. But I have no proof of anything," Dr. Parker replied. "The American Indians believed and still believe that their buried ancestors should not be disturbed. Some tribes don't even keep their possessions after they die. Some items are buried with them. Or sometimes they will burn them. Some tribes fear that evil things will happen to anyone who touches items belonging to a person that died."

"Do you think a spirit could have been following us?" asked Jane.

"Anything is possible," said Dr. Parker. "Not surprisingly in the field of Archaeology, I've heard many interesting stories. And it's one thing to dig up a kitchen area, but another to find bones. Whenever we discover human bones at a dig, we contact the authorities, in case we have discovered a cemetery. The tribe may want to move the bones to another location. We have to be careful to always show respect to buried ancestors. Different cultures feel differently about this, so it matters to us, whenever it matters to them."

"Ugh, enough dead talk. I guess we'll be going," said Peaches.

"Thanks for stopping by," said Dr. Parker. "I'll let you know what I find out about the item you brought in."

"Thanks, Dad," said Peaches.

"Thanks, Dr. Parker," said Jane, wishing they didn't have to leave yet. She enjoyed looking around the lab and hearing Dr. Parker talk about Archaeology.

Jane and Peaches headed back across the quad to their dorm room. "I hope nothing evil happens to you for touching that artifact," said Jane.

"Oh, ha ha," said Peaches.

"Well, something followed us out of the woods."

"No one followed us," said Peaches. "It was your imagination."

"Maybe," said Jane. "Maybe not."

"So, you're thinking of studying Archaeology?" asked Peaches, changing the subject. "I didn't know that."

"Maybe," said Jane. "That was kind of cool how you found that artifact on the side of the bluff, and they go on digs and come back and research all the items and make replicas for display. It sounds exciting!"

"Well, if you're going to do something for a career, you should be excited about it."

"I agree," said Jane. "I'm can't wait to find out about the thing you found."

CHAPTER THREE

GRAVEYARD RUN

THE NEXT MORNING, Jane was up early. "Are you sure you don't want to go running this morning with us? I don't have any classes until later," she asked Peaches, who was still in bed with her eyes closed.

"Too soon, Jane! Not a fan of early mornings," said Peaches, without opening her eyes. "I got up early with you just the other day to hike."

"Yes, you did, and it was fun," said Jane, as she pulled on her shorts.

"I don't get up early for just anyone, you know," said Peaches, groggily, as she put her pillow over her head.

"I appreciate that," said Jane, as she sat in the chair and finished putting on her running shoes. She strapped on her watch, and then pulled her long, dark hair back into a ponytail and added a multi-colored headband.

"See ya later." She grabbed her water bottle and headed outside to meet her cousin Ashley, and Ashley's dog and best pal, Edward.

Ashley is Jane's six-foot-tall cousin who is four years older than Jane. She is a gym warrior who likes any sport, lifts weights and likes to run for fun. Edward is a black Labrador Retriever that Ashley adopted when he was a three-year-old stray.

Ashley had persuaded Jane to start running with her over the summer, and now that Jane was living in the dorm, it was a good excuse to get together with her cousin. Jane was beginning to get used to it, and even started looking forward to running with Ashley.

Jane spotted Ashley across the quad, sitting on a bench, as soon as she emerged from the dormitory building. She was wearing her usual garb: a muscle tank top, basketball shorts, and a headband that resembles an American flag. Instead of her usual high-top basketball shoes, she was wearing running shoes today.

"Hey Jane, over here," Ashley called and waved. Edward jumped up and immediately started wagging his tail when he saw Jane coming towards them. Ashley held tight to his leash to keep him from bounding over to greet Jane.

"Good morning, Ashley. Good morning, Edward." Jane bent down and gave Edward a big hug around his neck while he licked and slobbered on her face. "Yuk," said Jane, as she wiped off her face onto her tee shirt sleeve.

"Guess how much I bench pressed this

morning?" said Ashley.

"Um, I dunno. 125?" replied Jane.

"135!" said Ashley. She grinned ear to ear.

"Wow, I can't even imagine that. Congrats!" said Jane.

"Yup. Ready to go?" said Ashley.

"Ready. I was thinking we could head down towards the community swimming pool and run on some trails around the burial mounds where that American Indian village was."

"Well, okay." Ashley shrugged. "It doesn't matter to me. C'mon, Edward," she said, as she tugged slightly on the leash. Edward immediately started trotting alongside Ashley.

As they ran along, Jane told Ashley about her hike with Peaches, and how they started at the other end of the serpent mound, but never finished the hike. She also told her about the artifact and the rescue on the bluff.

"Wowza," said Ashley. "That sounds crazy. It's a good thing it turned out well."

"Yeah, I was scared to death she would fall," said Jane.

"Well, she didn't, so try not to think about it," said Ashley. "You found a way to pull it off. Good for you."

Jane nodded in agreement, shuddering to think about it.

As they approached the burial mound near the swimming pool., Jane was struggling to keep up with Ashley. "I need to stop for a minute," said Jane. "I'm really thirsty and need to catch my breath." The girls stopped to drink some water.

"I remember when we used to hike here when we were kids," said Jane. It was now covered with a thick layer of dirt and grass and a picnic shelter. "I didn't really understand what this was at the time. I wanted to come back and see it again and understand more about it."

"I guess since I'm older, I probably understood more about it than you did," said Ashley.

"I was hoping you knew more about it," said Jane, nodding her head.

"This is what is considered the head of the serpent mound. It's where the village used to be," said Ashley. "People were finding all sorts of pottery, pipes, and arrowheads and primitive tools buried here," she explained. "They think this part is where ancient people were making pottery," she said, as she gestured to the area in front of them.

Ashley pointed towards the woods. "Then over there where it's all woods is where the cemetery is located. Some of the bones were only two feet deep, which is why they covered the whole area with a bunch of dirt and they don't allow anyone to dig here."

"Yeah, I remember some of this," said Jane.

"They found about 400 people buried in the cemetery over there. Just bones from hundreds of years ago. Back before cars and trains, people used the river for transportation. That's why so many people settled beside rivers and waterways," said

Ashley.

"That makes sense," nodded Jane. "It must have been a pretty large village if 400 people were buried here."

"Yeah, I guess so. They found some kitchen areas, hearths, and some cache-pits, which ancient people dug to store food. There were a lot of them, so there must have been a lot of people living in the village," said Ashley. "Or they could have lived here at different times."

"Sounds like it was a busy place," said Jane.

"I don't know why, but I always feel a little uncomfortable walking around here, which is why I'd rather run," said Ashley. "Maybe because it's a cemetery and even though no one is living here, I feel kinda like we're trespassing."

Jane said, "Do you hear that?"

"Hear what?" asked Ashley.

"It sort of sounds like a drum beat off in the distance. And chanting," said Jane.

"Mmmm, I'm not sure I hear anything like that," replied Ashley, looking around.

"Listen. It's very clear. Like tribal drum beats, and maybe singing," said Jane. She turned and walked a few steps toward the sound. "Now it sounds like it's coming from that way." She pointed in a different direction.

"I don't hear anything, but I feel like someone is following us. I keep looking behind me, but no one is there," said Ashley.

"Yeah, I feel like someone is watching us, but I

don't see anyone around here."

"It's kind of spooky," said Ashley. "I feel like someone doesn't like us running through here."

"Let's keep going," said Jane. "We can run along the mound by the river from here."

"Sounds good," agreed Ashley.

The girls and Edward ran steadily along the river towards the bluff until they reached the highest point. Ashley ran slower than she normally would so that Jane could keep up. They stopped at the top to look out over the river.

"I love this view," said Jane. "They should install a bench right here, so that people could sit for a while and maybe eat lunch here."

"That's a pretty good idea!" said Ashley. "They could add a vending machine too!"

Jane laughed. "Yeah, that would be handy."

"Maybe I'll suggest it to the park service," said Ashley. "Really, I might do that."

"Um, okay. Make sure they put some candy bars and snacks in it," said Jane. She chuckled.

"Will do," said Ashley. "I'm serious."

"Okay. Over there is where Peaches climbed down and found the artifact," said Jane, pointing to the ledge.

Ashley walked over to the ledge to take a look below. "That would have been a long drop if she fell," said Ashley, looking over the edge.

"Yeah, I know," said Jane.

"Hey look," said Ashley, pointing to part of a fallen tree. "I bet I can pick up that log." She walked over to the tree.

"It looks pretty heavy. It must be nearly six feet long," said Jane.

"Watch this," said Ashley, as she bent over and grabbed the middle of the log and hoisted it over her head like a barbell. "Tada!" she said.

"That's impressive," said Jane. "How long can you hold it up there?"

"A pretty long while," said Ashley. "But I'm ready to get going. I'm starting to cool down." She lowered the log close to the ground, and then let it go.

The girls started running again and picked up their speed along the trail. "You're doing a lot better with running than you were. I think you're making some progress," observed Ashley.

"I feel like I am, too," said Jane. "I'm beginning to really like it, even though it's not easy."

"Nothing easy is a good workout," said Ashley. "This is the best kind, because it's hard."

"I'll take your word for that," said Jane. "I think I'm starting to wear out now, though."

"I'm not surprised," said Ashley. "We ran a much longer way than you have before. It's easier when you can find interesting scenery. Good work!"

"Thanks," said Jane. "I'm about to drop."

"Let's head out this way to River Street, and we'll go back to the campus," said Ashley. They jogged slowly along the street until they reached the university campus.

"Thanks Ash, that was fun," said Jane. "We need to keep doing this. I think it's getting a little easier."

"Yeah, anytime. I love it!" said Ashley. "I can't wait until you're ready for your first 5K race."

"Race?" said Jane, with her eyebrows raised. "We'll see. Maybe."

Ashley laughed. "See ya later. C'mon Edward." She tugged on the leash.

"Bye, Ash. Bye, Edward," said Jane. She waved goodbye and walked back to her dormitory.

"I'm soooo hungry," she said when she walked in the door. She opened a bottle of water and drank all of it.

"There might be a brownie left," said Peaches, who was now awake and dressed.

"Good, maybe that will hold me until I can stop by the campus café before class," said Jane. "Running makes me hungry." She took the last brownie out of the container and ate it in two bites. Then she grabbed a banana from the basket on top of their small refrigerator and ate that, too.

"You might want to let your grandma know we ran out of brownies. You know, in case she wants to make more," laughed Peaches. "I'm going to meet up with some friends for coffee now," she said.

"You drink coffee?" said Jane.

"Only if it has enough sugar and caramel and other stuff in it," said Peaches.

"Ah, I see," said Jane, with a smile. "Have fun. See ya after classes today. I'm headed for the shower."

"See ya," said Peaches.

Later that day, Jane and Peaches met up back at their dorm room. They went together to the campus café for dinner and to check out all the groups and activity tables and get some information about what was available to join.

"So many options," said Peaches, as they walked back to their dorm room. "I'm not sure what to join. I did like the round robin tennis group. That would be fun, and no pressure. We could meet some people that like to play."

"Me too. I want to do it. I might want to join the team next year, so I need to keep playing," said Jane. "I'll have to look through all this info when we get back and see what else I might want to do."

CHAPTER FOUR

ATTACKED!

"JANE, JANE, WAKE UP," said Peaches, as she jostled Jane's shoulder early the next morning.

"Wha?" said Jane, as she rubbed her eyes, trying to open them. "What are you doing up before me this morning?" she asked.

"It's my dad," said Peaches. "Something happened in the Archaeology lab."

"What happened?" asked Jane.

"I'm not sure yet," said Peaches. "He said the police are there now. Will you come with me?"

"Of course," said Jane. "Give me a minute to get dressed."

Jane got dressed and accompanied Peaches to the Arts and Sciences Building, nervous about what might have happened. Why would Dr. Parker call Peaches so early? Something terrible must have happened, thought Jane.

Two police cars were parked in front of the Arts

and Sciences Building. There was a group of students standing around outside the building trying to see what was going on.

A police officer stopped the girls outside when they tried to enter the building. "You can't go in there," he said.

"But my dad is an Archaeology professor, and he is inside," Peaches protested.

"You still can't go in," the officer insisted. "You can wait out here for him."

"Is my dad okay?" she asked.

"Yes, he's fine. He was at home when it happened," said the officer.

"When what happened?" asked Peaches.

The officer didn't answer. Jane and Peaches looked at each other with their eyes wide, wondering what was so bad that he wouldn't tell them.

Jane realized she needed to be the calm one, since Peaches was worried about her dad. "We'll wait right here on the bench," said Jane. She could hear a siren getting louder, as she pulled Peaches by the arm toward the bench and they sat down. The ambulance pulled up to the building blasting its siren and then shut it off abruptly.

Two paramedics rushed into the building with a gurney and the policeman held the door open for them. Jane and Peaches waited silently on the bench. A few minutes later they emerged from the building with someone lying on the gurney. "That's Carl!" Peaches jumped up and pointed towards him.

"Is he alive?" asked Jane.

Peaches ran over to the gurney. "Carl, are you okay? What happened?" she asked, as the paramedics pushed the gurney toward the open ambulance door.

He opened his eyes. "I'm not sure," he answered weakly.

"He's alive!" said Peaches.

"That's a relief," said Jane.

"You're gonna be okay, Carl!" said Peaches. She patted him on the shoulder. "You hang in there!"

The paramedics lifted the gurney into the ambulance and one of them got in with him. The other paramedic shut the doors and got into the driver's seat and drove off with the siren blaring.

"Where's your mom?" asked Jane.

"She worked all night at the hospital. She doesn't get off work for another hour. That's why Dad called me to tell me that something happened in the lab and that he had to come over here. He couldn't reach her and wanted one of us to know where he went," said Peaches.

After the Arts and Sciences Building was cleared of police, Peaches and Jane were allowed to enter. They took the elevator to the second floor to Dr. Parker's office. The door was already open.

"Dad, what happened?" said Peaches, as soon as she spotted her dad. She ran to him and put her arms around him and held him tightly.

"Oh, hi sweetie," said Dr. Parker as he hugged her. "I didn't mean for you to come here," he said. "I just wanted to let you know what was going on."

"What IS going on?" she asked. "You weren't

clear on the phone. I saw them carry Carl out on a stretcher."

"They're taking him to the hospital, and hopefully he'll be okay," said Dr. Parker. "He was working late last night and someone broke in and hit him over the head with something. He was hurt pretty badly."

"Oh, wow," said Jane. "Was he knocked out?"

"Yes, apparently he was here all night, lying on the floor unconscious. The paramedics were able to revive him, though, which is a good sign. The security officer found him this morning when he was making his rounds."

"Why would someone do that?" asked Peaches.

"I don't know yet. Maybe to steal something? But we don't have anything valuable in here that I know about. The only thing I've noticed that's gone is those sand paintings that I showed you the other day. They were on that shelf over there.

"It looks like a lot of drawers are open," Peaches observed.

"Someone was obviously looking for something. I haven't looked in the drawers yet. I'll need to do a full inventory and see if anything else is missing."

"Can we help?" said Jane.

"I wish you could," said Dr. Parker. "But since you're not Archaeology students, you won't know how to handle the artifacts. I'll need to get some of the students in here to help. Everything has been documented in some way, even the new items from the summer."

"As long as you're okay, Dad," said Peaches.

"I am. I was at home when it happened," he said. "I wish Carl had been at home, too. I can't believe this happened to him. I hope he'll be alright."

"Maybe you can ask Mom to check on him," said Peaches. "I assume they took him to the West Midland Hospital?"

"Probably," said Dr. Parker. "I'll talk to her later today and ask her to see if she can find out how he's doing. I need to call his parents right away."

"Do you have any photos of the missing sand paintings?" asked Jane.

"Well, yes," said Dr. Parker. "We would have taken some initial photos at the dig before we packed things up."

"Can we get a copy?" asked Jane. "I'd like to see if I can find out anything about them at the library."

"Well, I guess so," said Dr. Parker. He walked over to his computer and started typing. "I just sent them to the printer. I'll go get them." He walked over to the printer and pulled off a few sheets of paper and put them in a folder.

"Here you go," said Dr. Parker. "Let me know if you find out anything. I'm pleased to see your interest in Archaeology, Jane."

"Thanks, Dr. Parker," said Jane, as she took the folder. "I just want to help find out why someone attacked Carl."

"You girls probably need to get to class. There's nothing you can do here. I have some phone calls to make."

"Okay, then," said Peaches. "We'll go, but let me know what you find out."

"I will, sweetie. I promise," said Dr. Parker.

Peaches and Jane left the Arts and Sciences Building and were walking back to their dorm room.

"Let's go get some breakfast," said Peaches. "I can't go back to bed now and I'm hungry."

"Why don't we walk to the Village Café?" said Jane. "I don't want to go back to our room yet either."

As soon as the girls walked into the café, Jane was captivated by the smell of bacon cooking and coffee brewing. "Mmm, that smells great," she said.

"It sure does," said Peaches. "I think I want some pancakes and bacon."

"That sounds good," said Jane. The Village Café was small and homey, with blue checkered curtains in the windows and solid blue matching tablecloths. There was a candle centerpiece on each table. The sign at the door said SEAT YOURSELF. A couple of people were already sitting at the counter eating and several tables were full.

"It's pretty busy in here this morning. I hope service isn't too slow. I have a class at nine," said Peaches.

They sat at a table by the window. Jane set the folder on the table. A server wearing a nametag that said 'Molly' came over and took their orders pretty quickly. Jane assumed she was probably another college student.

"I'm going to see what I can find out about

these sand paintings," said Jane, as she opened the folder and pulled out the papers. Peaches picked up one of them and looked at it.

"I wonder what these symbols mean," said Peaches. Jane looked at the paper that Peaches was holding.

"I couldn't even guess," said Jane. "But I'll ask my friend Nate to help me research them and see what we can find out."

"You don't have to do that," said Peaches. "My dad will work on it as soon as he can get to it."

"I know, but he has to go through all the inventory and figure out what's missing, and that might take a while. I think they're really interesting, and maybe it would help them figure out who attacked Carl if we can find out more about them. The sooner the better," said Jane.

"I'd like whoever hurt Carl to get caught as soon as possible," agreed Peaches. She furrowed her brow and gritted her teeth and said, "I'd like to give them a piece of my mind. So, anything you can find out would be great."

"I'm going to do what I can," said Jane, nodding to reassure her.

Jane got up to go to the restroom, while Peaches checked her phone for messages. There was one from her mom, asking if she wanted to come to dinner one night this week. Her mom had sent the message the night before, but somehow she hadn't seen it until now. Peaches was startled when she looked up to see a man had grabbed the folder from the table and ran.

"Hey!" she yelled, as he ran out the front door. Peaches jumped up and ran to the door, but he was gone.

Jane came back from the restroom, just as Peaches sat back down at the table. "Where's the folder?" she asked.

"Some guy ran up and grabbed it and ran out the door," said Peaches. "I tried to chase after him, but he was out of sight."

"What the heck?" said Jane. "Why would someone steal the folder? Did you see what he looked like?"

Peaches yawned and thought for a minute. "I don't know. Let me see. He had short brown hair and light skin, kind of average size, wearing jeans and a maybe a blue shirt. He might have been wearing glasses, and I think he had a short beard. It was so quick, I barely saw him."

The server came over to the table. "Is everything alright?" she asked.

"Did you see the guy that grabbed our folder off this table?" asked Jane.

"Well, yeah, I did. I waited on him. He was sitting at the table behind you. And he just ran out without paying."

"He was sitting right there?" asked Jane, pointing to the table behind her.

"Yes," said the server.

"Thanks," said Jane.

"Your food should be ready in a few minutes,"

said the server. She walked away.

"That guy was close enough to have heard everything we said about the sand paintings," said Jane.

"Yeah, he was," said Peaches.

"I'll stop back by the Arts and Sciences Building today after my first class and see if I can get another copy from your dad," said Jane. "This time I'll take a picture of them on my cell phone, so I don't have to carry a folder around."

"That's a good idea," said Peaches.

After breakfast, the girls walked back to their dorm room. Peaches looked around, as she thought someone was following them.

"Did you see anyone behind us?" she whispered to Jane. "I feel like we're being followed."

Jane tried to look around without being obvious. "There is a guy back there in a blue shirt and jeans. Let's turn down this way and see if he follows."

"That looks like the guy that took the folder. Still following," said Peaches.

"Let's go in the Commons Building and see if we lose him," said Jane.

They entered the building and then went out the side door. "Did we lose him?" asked Jane.

"Looks like it," said Peaches. "Let's hurry back to the dorm, before he realizes we're not coming back out the same door."

"Safe and sound," said Peaches, as they entered their dorm room.

"I'll text my dad and make sure he doesn't have

some FBI agent following me around to protect me," said Jane.

> Jane:HI DAD
> Dad::HI
> Jane:ARE YOU STILL HAVING ANYONE FOLLOW ME?
> Dad: NO, WHY?
> Jane:JUST BEING PARANOID I GUESS, NVR MND
> Dad: LET ME KNOW IF THERE IS
> Jane:I WILL

"I'll see you later this afternoon after classes," said Jane.

"See ya," said Peaches, as she headed out to class.

CHAPTER FIVE
RESEARCH AT THE LIBRARY

JANE DIDN'T WAKE UP until almost nine o'clock in the morning. She didn't usually have the luxury of sleeping that late.

"I'm going to the library this morning to see what I can find out about the sand paintings. My friend Nate is working today and he's really good at research," said Jane.

"Was he the one that helped you track down that painting from your grandparents' house?" asked Peaches.

"Yeah, he's really good at it. I learned a lot from him when we were trying to find out more about that painting, but I don't know anything about sand paintings," said Jane. "I never even heard of a sand painting before now. I know he'll be able to figure out something about them."

"Good luck, then. I have a paper to write for class," said Peaches. "I'll be here for the next few hours."

Jane walked to the library, since the university campus was close by. She enjoyed an opportunity to be outdoors whenever possible. She had barely driven her blue Jeep Cherokee, which she had named Bernice, since she started living on campus. Everything she had needed so far was close enough to walk.

When Jane reached the library, she looked up at the old building and got the same happy feeling she had always had gotten when she was here. She gazed around at the beautiful old architecture of the building, which was hundreds of years old. It was originally a stagecoach stop, according to the sign on the front lawn.

Jane loved breathing in the woody smell of old books when she walked in the front door. She had many memories of her visits to this library as a child, and more recently when her friend, Nate, was helping her do research over the summer.

She walked up to the front desk where Nate was helping another patron, and quietly waited until he was free.

"Hi Nate," said Jane.

Nate turned his head to look. "Well, hi there stranger," said Nate, with a big smile. "I haven't seen you since I had dinner at your grandparents' house."

Jane smiled warmly as she gazed at his dreamy ocean blue eyes and dark wavy hair. "They really loved meeting you," said Jane.

"They are really nice. You're lucky to have

them, especially living so close by," said Nate. "What brings you here today?"

"Research," said Jane. "And you're the best at it."

"Great! What are we researching today?" said Nate.

"Sand paintings," replied Jane.

"Sand paintings?" said Nate. "I don't know much of anything about that, so this should be interesting."

"Glad to hear it," replied Jane. "I have some photos on my phone, which I will send to you. I had printed copies but someone stole them right off the table, while Peaches and I were at the Village Café."

Nate raised his eyebrows. "Stole them?" he asked. "Jane, what have you gotten yourself into?"

"I hope nothing like last time," said Jane. "Do you remember meeting my friend Peaches?"

"Yeah," Nate nodded. "I remember her."

"Some sand paintings were stolen from her father's Archaeology lab at the university... and the teaching assistant was also found unconscious in the lab at the same time," said Jane.

"Jane, you need to be careful," warned Nate. "And how do you have photos of them if they were stolen?"

"They were from a dig out West this summer. There were photos taken of them before they were stolen."

"Oh, I see," said Nate.

"I just want to know more about them and what

the symbols on them mean, so we can understand why someone might steal them," said Jane.

"We can probably figure that out," said Nate.

"I'm sending them to you now," said Jane, looking down at her cell phone.

"Got 'em," said Nate. "Okay, let's see. I can't tell what kind of material these are made from. But I can do some research and see what I find."

"Anything you can find out would be great. But I especially would like to find out about the symbols. But maybe they're valuable or something and that's why they were stolen. I just don't know. Somebody might have tried to kill Carl for them. I don't know what else they stole, but it's important that we find out everything we can."

"That makes sense. I'm happy to help however I can," said Nate. "It might take me a few days, though."

"That's fine," said Jane. "I really appreciate your help and I'm sure Dr. Parker will, too."

Nate looked up. "I see some patrons at the desk, and need to go help them. I'll let you know what I find," said Nate. "Oh, one more thing… I'm going with some friends tonight to that fifties-style burger place on Main Street for some burgers and sand volleyball. Do you want to go with me?"

"Yes, I'd love to go," Jane replied with a big grin. "I've haven't been there yet and it looks like fun."

"I'll come by the dorm and get you at 6:30. Is that okay?" he said, as he started walking toward the main desk.

"Sounds great! Thanks again for your help," said Jane.

Jane was still smiling to herself when she left the library to head back to her dorm room. She was excited to go out with Nate tonight and meet some of his friends.

She had just stepped outside of the library, when she saw a man that looked like the one that had followed her and Peaches from the Village Café – the one that stole the photos of the sand paintings. He was just leaving the front of the library, when she came outside.

Jane ducked behind a large maple tree, so that he wouldn't see her when he looked around. She wondered if he had followed her to the library. But why? He already had the photos.

He crossed the main street at the intersection. Jane started following him, taking care to duck behind utility poles and trees whenever she thought he was looking her way. She also crossed the main intersection, and watched him walk quickly down the tree-lined street.

Two men in blue jeans and boots were standing beside a dirty white pickup truck that was parked under a tree on the street. One of them was wearing a cowboy hat. When they saw him, they both climbed into the truck. When the man that Jane was following reached the truck, he got into the driver's side. Jane tried to see the license plate, but she was only close enough to see that it was from New Mexico. The truck drove away.

Hmmm, thought Jane. I'll bet that was the guy that stole the photos and followed us back to school. I wonder what they are up to.

Jane ran back to the dorm room to tell Peaches about the men, but Peaches had already gone to class. She would tell her later.

Jane locked the door and settled into her comfy chair to write a paper for her English class. She tried to concentrate on what she was writing, but her mind kept drifting back to the men from New Mexico. "What could they want?" she thought. Eventually, she finished her paper, but it took much longer than it should have.

Later that evening, Jane went to Rock Around the Clock, the burger place with Nate, where they met up with some of his friends. When she got home, Peaches was curled up in a comfy chair studying.

"How was it?" asked Peaches, looking up from her book.

"It was fun," said Jane. "I've never played volleyball in the sand before, so that was cool. His friends were nice, too."

"Good," said Peaches. "Nate seems like a nice guy."

"He really is," said Jane. "I'm glad I met him. He's a lot of fun. And competitive, too. I'm not sure why that surprised me, but he's really good at volleyball."

"His sister plays softball, doesn't she?" said

Peaches.

"That's true. He may be more sports-minded than I realized. I used to see him at a lot of her games, when my friend Rachel was on her team," Jane agreed. "Maybe he was there just as much for the enjoyment of sports, as he was to support his sister."

"Sounds like it," agreed Peaches.

"Long day," said Jane, as she gathered her towel, shampoo, and pajamas. "I'm going to grab a shower. I'll try to be quiet so you can study."

"Thanks," said Peaches, giving her the thumbs-up sign.

CHAPTER SIX
HOSPITAL VISIT

PEACHES HAD A SURPRISE for Jane for the morning. She set up a doubles match on the university tennis courts with some new friends from school, Michelle and Robin.

Jane was pleased for an opportunity to play some tennis. She hadn't played at all since school started, and hadn't even thought about setting up a match yet. She was happy to be playing.

"It's great to be back on the court again," said Peaches, bouncing around the court and swinging her racquet around.

"It sure is," agreed Jane.

The four girls played two sets of doubles, and each side won a set. Rather than play a third set, they decided to play a nine-point tie-break to determine the winner. Peaches and Jane won the tie-break 5-2.

The girls all shook hands across the net when they were finished playing.

"Thanks for playing today," said Peaches.

"That was really fun," said Jane.

"Let us know anytime you want to play," said Michelle. "I think we're all pretty evenly matched, so that made it fun."

"Will do," said Peaches.

Jane and Peaches sat down on the bench with the other girls to change their shoes and grab a drink before leaving. "That felt good," said Jane. "Want some peanuts?" Peaches held out her hand and Jane poured some of her peanuts into it.

"Thanks," said Peaches. She started munching on them. Two boys in tee shirts and shorts approached the court with tennis bags, so the girls got up to leave and let the boys have the court.

After they bade their friends goodbye and walked across the quad to their dorm room, Jane wondered how Carl was doing.

"Have you heard anything about Carl?" said Jane. "How is he doing?"

"Mom said he's doing a little better each day. He can have visitors now," said Peaches.

"Really? Do you want to go see him?" Jane asked.

"That's a good idea," said Peaches. "I don't have a class for a few hours if you want to go now."

"Let's put our tennis gear in the room and shower first," said Jane.

"And eat something," Peaches added.

Jane microwaved some Ramen noodles and ate a couple of mozzarella cheese sticks, and Peaches made herself a peanut butter and strawberry jelly sandwich for lunch, before they headed out.

As they walked to the West Midland Hospital, Jane kept looking around to make sure no one was following them. She kept an eye out for white pickup trucks, too.

"What are you doing?" said Peaches. "You look like an owl with your head swiveling all around like that."

Jane laughed. "I'm just nervous about being followed after what's happened. I'm also watching out for that pickup truck from New Mexico."

"I don't see anyone around today," said Peaches.

"Good," said Jane.

They reached the hospital entrance and walked into the lobby. "I haven't been here for a while," said Jane. "I'm trying to remember when I was here last."

"I come here a lot," said Peaches. "But only to talk to my mom. Her office is on the third floor in Cardiology."

Jane felt butterflies in her stomach going every which way. She was nervous about seeing Carl. She last saw him on the gurney being rushed into the ambulance and he was barely conscious. He had looked pretty bad. But she really wanted to see him now, so she could get that image out of her head and see him looking better.

"Let's stop in the gift shop and get him something. We can't go in empty-handed," said Jane. "Balloons?"

"Yeah, balloons sound good," nodded Peaches.

The girls bought some balloons that said Get Well Soon. "Do you know Carl's room number?" asked Jane.

"537," said Peaches. "He's out of Intensive Care now and in a private room."

"Yikes, he was in there for a while then," said Jane.

"He was hurt pretty badly, from what I heard," said Peaches.

They hopped on the elevator to the fifth floor and found Carl's room. Peaches poked her head in the door first and lightly knocked. "Hello?"

"C'mon in," said Carl. "It's open." The girls entered the room. Jane braced herself for how Carl might look.

Peaches presented the balloons to Carl. "We brought you something," she said.

"Thanks," said Carl weakly. "That was nice of you."

Jane let herself look at Carl. He looked like he had been punched in the eye, as well as knocked over the head. His head was wrapped in gauze, and his eye was purple and bruised. "How are you feeling?" she asked.

"Like I was knocked in the head," said Carl. "But better than I felt last week."

"So, you're improving?" said Peaches.

"Yes, that's what they tell me."

"Good," said Jane. "You hang in there. Is there anything you need or anything we can do for you?"

"Hmmm, can't think of anything right now," said Carl. "But thanks. My parents have been here every day, so they've been taking care of things for me."

"That's good," said Peaches. "I'm glad they were able to come and stay."

"Yeah, they were pretty freaked out at first, but they are calming down as I get better. It's not something they ever imagined would happen to me at school."

"I guess not," said Peaches.

"They're talking about releasing me soon," he said.

"That's good," said Jane. "That must mean you're doing better."

"Yeah, I guess it does. Have you heard anything about who did this?" asked Carl. "Nobody is telling me anything."

"No, we don't know either," said Peaches. "Someone stole those two sand paintings and ransacked the drawers. I don't know what else they took. My dad is doing an inventory to find out if anything else is missing. Jane is trying to find out more about the sand paintings to see if there are any clues about who it was and why."

"Thanks girls. Let me know what you find out," said Carl.

"We will," said Jane. "If we can find out anything."

"Do you remember anything that happened?" asked Peaches.

Carl sighed. "All I remember is that I was putting things away in the storage room, and when I came out to the lab, there were a couple of guys in there digging through the drawers. They must have turned the lights off, because they were on before I went into the storage room. I couldn't see them very well. I was caught by surprise, so I wasn't sure what to do. I thought about ducking back out of the lab and calling the police, but they saw me. So, I started to yell 'hey,' and then someone grabbed me by the shoulder from behind and turned me around and punched me in the face. That's all I remember."

"Do you remember what they looked like?" Jane asked.

"Not really, just some guys. It was kind of dark with the lights off, but there were two of them digging through the drawers, and apparently one behind me. I would swear I locked the door to the lab when I came in that night."

"Wow," said Peaches. "That's a terrible thing to happen to you."

"Yeah," agreed Jane. She was imagining Carl trying to defend himself against three guys. He was kind of a small nerdy guy that didn't look very athletic or strong. Jane thought it was lucky that he had survived the attack.

"You let us know if we can do anything for you," said Peaches.

"I will," said Carl. "Thanks for the balloons and for coming to see me."

"Take care, Carl," said Jane, as they left the

room. They took the elevator down to the lobby.

"Do you want to stop by and see your dad on the way back?" asked Jane.

"Um, I don't know, not really," said Peaches. "Why?"

"I dunno, I just thought if my dad was on campus, I would want to see him whenever I could," said Jane. "That's okay, though, if you don't really want to."

"When are you supposed to hear from your dad again?" asked Peaches.

"I'm not sure," said Jane. "Since he works undercover for the FBI now, he can't come home or call whenever he wants. I just have to be patient and wait to hear from him. I can text him, though."

"Well, uh, my mom invited me over to dinner tonight, if you wanna come with me," said Peaches, suddenly realizing how much Jane missed her dad.

"Do you think she'd mind?" asked Jane.

"Nah, I'll just text her and let her know you're coming."

"Thanks!" said Jane, with a smile.

The girls walked back to the university and across the quad to their dorm. "I feel better now that I've seen that Carl is improving," said Peaches.

"Me too," said Jane. "I was a little scared about how he would look since he still isn't out of the hospital."

"At least he's safe in there," said Peaches.

"Yeah, I didn't think of that," said Jane.

Neither of them had classes that day, so they

both spent the afternoon on homework after their busy morning. When they were both finished, they went to visit Peaches' parents at their house for dinner.

Dr. Parker, Peaches' mom, and Dr. Parker, Peaches' dad, both seemed pleased to have Jane join them for dinner. It was still warm enough to have dinner out on the patio, and Jane enjoyed getting away from cafeteria food and spending the evening with them. Dr. Parker (mom) was a great cook. After dinner, they played Yahtzee for a while, before Jane and Peaches had to get back to the dorm.

It was a beautiful Fall evening and Jane and Peaches walked back to the campus after dinner. "That was really fun," said Jane. "Thanks for inviting me."

"I'm glad you had fun," Peaches replied.

"Well, I love hearing your dad's stories. He's been to a lot of different places," said Jane.

"Yeah, he used to be gone a lot like your dad, like on digs, you know? But now that he started teaching, I get to see him all the time. Except he does the student dig every summer. I miss him when he's gone."

"Well, it's nice having your parents around, even though they're not my parents," said Jane.

"You have your grandparents. They live close by."

"Oh, of course. I love seeing them, too," said Jane. "But I still like hanging out with your parents."

"I wish my mom would stop pressuring me to become a doctor," Peaches complained. "She says the world needs more Black doctors. But Dad understands and says that I should do something I'm passionate about. I don't want to be a doctor. Even though it would have been awesome to share that with my mom, it's just not me."

"I can see that," said Jane, nodding.

"I want to be a photographer. But Mom says that's not practical. But it's what I'm passionate about," said Peaches.

"Yeah, I get it," said Jane. "I'm trying to figure out what I want, too."

CHAPTER SEVEN
WHO PUSHED JANE?

"NATE SAID HE has some information for me, so I'm off to the library this morning before class," said Jane, while putting on her shoes. She stood up and grabbed her notebook and a pen to take with her.

Peaches covered her head with her pillow. "Have fun," she mumbled.

Jane walked towards the library. She reached the main crosswalk and pushed the button for the light to cross the street. She felt a hand on her back push her from behind really hard and she found herself out in the street in front of an oncoming car. She managed to stop herself and get back on the sidewalk. She breathed a sigh of relief, grabbing the light pole with one hand and holding her hand over her heart. She looked around to see who pushed her but no one was there.

Jane gathered her wits, and pushed the button for the walk light again. She looked around to make sure no one was behind her. The light changed to WALK and she walked quickly across the street.

When she arrived at the library, Jane was feeling a little jittery. She saw Nate helping a patron and waved to him and went to sit at a table.

When he was finished, he came over and sat down. "What happened to you?" he said. "You look shaken up."

"I am a little," said Jane. "Someone shoved me in front of a car back at the crosswalk."

"Shoved you? Or bumped you?" said Nate.

"It felt like a shove, and when I looked around, there wasn't even anyone there."

"That's odd," said Nate. "Just be careful with this sand painting thing. I can't imagine why anyone would steal your folder or push you in the street over it, but just pay attention to your surroundings."

"I will, I promise," said Jane. She held up three fingers. "Scout's honor." She smiled.

"Hey, you're not the Eagle Scout. I am," said Nate.

"I know," chuckled Jane. "But I don't have a thing like that. I wish I did."

Nate smiled. "Sit tight for a minute. I'll be right back." He went over to the customer service desk and pulled out a notebook from under it and came back to sit at the table.

"I wanted to show you what I found out about sand paintings," he said, as he opened his notebook. "They are created for healing ceremonies by some tribes. The ceremony is called a 'sing' and it is considered sacred and not shared with outsiders."

"A sing?" asked Jane. "Do they sing?"

"Yes, as a matter of fact," said Nate. "They sing a lot. When someone is sick, they say it is caused by evil forces. So a healing ceremony is performed to cleanse the person of any evil and bring blessing to him or her. They attack anything evil with rituals."

"That makes sense," said Jane.

"Supernatural beings are invited to come to the person and to the whole tribe and bring healing. Chants and sacred objects are used, such as prayer sticks and sand paintings."

"Now we're getting somewhere!" said Jane.

"The sand painting is created by several people who sprinkle dry sand colored with natural pigments. It's a form of an altar. The person sits on it, and a medicine man performs all sorts of rituals."

"It must be bigger than the ones that were found, then," said Jane.

"Yes, a lot bigger. A sand painting covers the entire floor. There are a number of different chants that can be performed by the medicine man. They have to know lots of songs, and the order of them, and they need to be able to plan and instruct everyone that is part of the healing ceremony including how to construct the sand painting. It can take years for the medicine man to learn how to do all this."

"That sounds very different from these two paintings," said Jane.

"It is," said Nate. "They never create anything permanent with sacred sand paintings. Anything created that is permanent, such as Peaches' dad found, would be a commercial craft. It isn't related at all to these rituals. Commercial sand painting was started to earn income and has nothing to do with healing or ceremonies."

"So, these were probably created just to sell?" said Jane.

"Yes, but it is believed that something really bad could happen to the person that creates a permanent sand painting, like a disaster or even death. It might even affect the tribe, if a sand painting is made in a permanent way."

"So, then why would they do it?" asked Jane.

"I don't know how many people feel that way, or how strongly they feel about it. It could be that entire tribes feel a certain way about it, or maybe some members in a tribe have different perspectives. There are so many different tribes and clans, you really can't lump their beliefs together. They're individuals like anyone else."

"Hmmm," said Jane.

"Sources of income have been limited on the reservations, and people need to eat and family ties are important. People don't want to leave the reservation to earn an income if they don't have to. Their families try to stay close together as much as possible."

"That's understandable," nodded Jane.

"Eventually there was some acceptance of this practice over 100 years ago – you know, creating the paintings to sell. There might still be some conflict in the way people feel about it."

"So, if this kind of sand painting has been around over 100 years, there are probably a lot of them around. I wonder why these two were hidden inside a cave, though," said Jane. "Dr. Parker said it didn't make sense to him, why someone would create them and then hide them."

"Yeah, that does seem strange," said Nate. "Maybe someone hid them in the cave just to get rid of them, because they believed they would cause harm. I tried to find out something about these specific ones, but couldn't find anything."

"What about the symbols on the sand paintings? Were you able to find anything out about them?" asked Jane.

"No, I came up empty on the symbols. I have no idea what they mean, and I don't know where else to look."

"Drat," said Jane.

"There just isn't a lot of written information that can help us with this," said Nate. "I think you're going to need to find someone who knows about this stuff. So much of this kind of history is oral, and learned through storytelling and from elders. It's not written down anywhere that I can find."

"Who would I ask?" said Jane.

"I was looking into that, too," said Nate. "There's a tribal museum out West that's really amazing and has artifacts from a number of different areas and tribes. You might be able to find something out from the curator there. I think it's a good place to start," said Nate. "It's called Yellowglen Tribal

Museum."

"Out West?" said Jane. "That sounds like a road trip."

"It does, and I'd love to go on one, but I have to work and can't get away anytime soon," said Nate.

"Too bad you can't go. That would have been fun," said Jane. "Do you have the address?"

"Yes, I wrote it right here for you. I wish I could find out more."

"You found out a lot," said Jane. "And I really appreciate all you've done."

"You know I love researching stuff," said Nate. "I was happy to do it."

"And I appreciate that, too," said Jane, smiling.

"You know, I'd like to see you again sometime when we're not researching something. Like a date, with just the two of us?" said Nate.

"That sounds good," said Jane. "If I go on a road trip out West, it'll have to wait until I get back. Is that okay?"

"It'll have to be," Nate sighed. Just then, he noticed a couple of people approaching the desk. He got up from the table. "I'm going to have to go help them," he said.

"Thanks Nate," said Jane. "As usual, you've been a great help. I guess I'd better get to class. And we're on for when I get back. See ya later."

"Bye, Jane," said Nate. "Be careful."

CHAPTER EIGHT
ROAD TRIP

PEACHES AND ASHLEY were both on board with a road trip out West. The next Monday was the start of Fall Break at school, so they left on Saturday morning. Ashley hadn't started her new job yet, and was happy to go on an adventure.

The girls loaded their backpacks in Ashley's Jeep. "Off we go," said Ashley, as she pulled out of the university parking lot.

"What state are we going to?" asked Peaches.

"New Mexico," said Jane.

"Don't worry," said Ashley. "We won't need a passport, although it'll seem like we've gone to another country since it's so far away and looks so different from Ohio."

"It'll go fast," said Jane. "There's so much to see on the way there."

"So what's in New Mexico exactly?" asked Peaches.

"There's a tribal museum near the dig where your dad found those sand paintings. It's the closest one and seems like they might have some, or may be able to interpret the symbols on them. We can talk to the curator and work from there. They study this kind of stuff and should know something."

"Good enough for me," said Peaches. "ROAD TRIP!" she yelled, with her fist in the air. She plopped into the back seat. "Right, Edward?" she said as she looked over at the dog. He wagged his tail and settled into the seat next to her.

The girls arrived late at night and checked into their hotel. They were exhausted from the long drive and went straight to bed.

The next morning, they got up early and went to the Yellowglen Tribal Museum. "That was a long drive just to get to this place," said Ashley. "I hope it was worth it and they actually have some info."

"We'll know soon," said Jane, as she got out of the Jeep.

"You stay here, boy," said Ashley to Edward. Edward wagged his tail and laid back down on the back seat and whimpered.

They went inside the entrance and looked around. "This museum is bigger than I imagined. Look at all the cool stuff," said Peaches.

"There's an information desk," said Ashley, pointing across the way. The girls headed over to the desk.

"Excuse me," said Jane. "May we speak to the curator?"

"Do you have an appointment with him?" said the girl behind the counter.

"No, I didn't think of that," said Jane, sounding disappointed. She wasn't looking forward to having to be pushy, but they had driven a long way, and she was hoping she would be able to get him to talk to her.

"I'll see if he's available," said the girl.

"Please tell him it's really important, and that we just drove here all the way from Ohio to see him," said Jane.

"Got it." The girl shrugged her shoulders and walked away.

About ten minutes later, the girl returned with the curator. Jane was relieved.

"Hello," he said, offering his hand. "I'm Jordan Crowfoot. I'm the curator here." Jane shook his hand.

"I'm Jane Teaberry, and this is my friend Peaches Parker, and my cousin, Ashley Fink. We drove here from Ohio, hoping you can help us with some information about a sand painting."

"A sand painting?" he said. "I haven't seen many of those, but I'll try to answer your questions."

"Thanks," said Jane. "We really appreciate it. You have a lot of great items here. Are they from different tribes?"

"Yes," said Jordan. "There are a number of tribes in the area. Some of the items were willed to us by people who had collected them in various ways, others were found in excavations, and some were purchased from tribes who needed the money for food and daily living expenses."

"That's sad," said Peaches.

"Yes, it is," said Jordan. "I don't know how well known it is, but these tribes were forced over decades into situations that don't really allow them to thrive and prosper. It's a shame. I don't feel great about how some of the items came to us, but I feel like we need this cultural center to help the younger tribe members understand their own heritage and customs, so this knowledge and understanding doesn't get lost."

"So, you're doing your part for your people, by helping them learn about their heritage?" said Peaches. "That's commendable."

"Thanks. I don't want the traditions and knowledge to get lost," Jordan explained. "So much has been lost already."

"I think that's important, too," said Jane. "I'm glad you're doing this."

"You wouldn't even believe what these tribes have lived through over the last few hundred years. But they're survivors. They get beaten down and keep on going. What questions did you have for me?" asked Jordan.

"The reason why we came here is that Peaches' dad is an Archaeology professor at West Midland University. They were out near here for an excavation over the summer, and found a couple of sand paintings. We were hoping you could tell us the meaning of some of the symbols on them."

"They found sand paintings?" he asked, looking perplexed.

"Yes, they were in a cave. They brought them back to Ohio."

"Do you have them with you?" he said.

"Right here on my phone," said Jane. She handed him her phone.

"You know that these sand paintings are not sacred, right? Sacred sand paintings are not permanent. They are made on the ground and used for healing ceremonies, and they are destroyed at the end of the ceremony. These would have been created just to sell as a craft."

"Yes, we do know that. However, someone broke into the Archaeology lab and seriously attacked a student and stole them. He's lucky to be alive. So, we're trying to find out what's so important about them."

"Wow, I'm so sorry to hear that. Is the student okay?"

"I think he will be," said Jane. "We heard he's improving. We just don't know if they'll come back, or if anyone else is in danger. We don't know what if anything else is missing yet. This is just one avenue we thought we could investigate to find out what's going on. Peaches' dad works in that lab all the time, and so do some of the students. We don't know if it's a safe place anymore."

"I see," said Jordan. "I don't know if the symbols will be meaningful, because I don't know why these were created. This symbol here looks like a location, maybe a mountain, but I'm not really sure where it is. This one over here looks like it indicates a battle. That probably isn't a lot of help."

"I really appreciate you trying," said Jane.

"You know, there is someone that might be able to interpret these. She's a sort of spiritual advisor, medicine woman. She knows pretty much everything about everything. Her name is Hehewuti."

"Do you think she would talk to us?" asked Ashley.

"I don't know. She might, if you are willing to go to her. She lives on a sacred mountain near here. She doesn't have an address and really isn't on a map, but I can give you directions to find her."

"How near?" asked Jane.

"About 50 miles away," said Jordan.

"That's not bad, considering how far we've come," said Ashley, nodding to Jane. "It'll take less than an hour to get there."

"Can you call her and ask if she'll see us?" asked Jane.

"No, sorry, she doesn't have a phone. You'll just have to take your chances and show up and ask if she'll talk to you. But I feel sure she'll know what this means. I'll write down the directions."

"Okay, great. Thanks for your help," said Jane.

Jordan handed the directions to Jane. "Good luck," he said. "Feel free to look around. You can learn a lot here about tribal life."

"Thanks Jordan."

They looked around at a few of the exhibits.

"Don't forget Edward is in the car," said Ashley.

"Oh, right, we better go," agreed Jane.

"Right behind you," said Peaches.

The girls headed out to the parking lot. Edward jumped up happily when he saw them. "What's that?" asked Peaches, pointing to the windshield.

"Ha! I've been ducked," said Ashley. She reached over and grabbed it from where it was wedged beside the windshield wiper.

"Why would there be a rubber duck on your windshield?" asked Peaches.

"Someone likes my Jeep. If you like a Jeep, you leave a duck. I'll add it to my collection," she said as she set it on the dashboard with several other different colored ducks. "I have a bag of them in the glove box. If you see a cool Jeep, we can duck them."

"Ohhh, I see. I wondered why you had ducks scattered on your dashboard," said Peaches. "Cool!"

"Let's go to the sacred mountain," said Ashley, as she pulled out onto the road.

CHAPTER NINE

THE SACRED MOUNTAIN

IT WAS LATE MORNING when the girls set out to find the sacred mountain. The sky was clear and the sun was hot. Even though it was Fall, it was extremely warm in New Mexico.

They weren't sure what they might encounter or how long it might take, so they packed plenty of snacks and water in the Jeep for the long drive. They stopped at a gas station and filled up the tank. Jane bought a paper map of the area.

They drove along a straight two-lane road for about thirty miles, hardly seeing any cars. They saw mile after mile of desert with a mountain backdrop, as they drove along. Cacti were strung along in between grass clumps.

"Let's keep an eye on the gas gauge," said Jane. "I don't wanna run out of gas out here in No Man's Land."

"We have plenty for now," said Ashley, who

was driving at the time. Peaches had fallen asleep in the backseat with Edward. He was sprawled across the seat with his head in her lap.

"I guess we got her up too early today," said Jane. "Hopefully a little nap will make up for it." She spread the paper map out in front of her.

"I was surprised you can still buy a paper map these days," said Ashley, looking over at the map. "Can you see how much farther it is?"

"About 20 more miles," said Jane. "And there is a white pickup truck coming up behind us now, so there's at least one other person out here in the desert. I don't know if that's the same one I saw back in West Midland." The truck had been gaining on them, but now started slowing down.

Ashley slowed down to let the truck pass, but it stayed behind them, maintaining the same distance, even when she sped back up. "Looks like they're staying back there," she observed.

"There is a little side road up ahead," said Jane, looking at the map. It curves around a little, and then you can get back on this road."

"Let me know when you see it," said Ashley.

"It's right up there," said Jane, pointing to the road.

Ashley maintained her speed until they almost reached the road and then abruptly turned off and sped up. The pickup truck looked like it hit the brakes and tried to slow down, but was too fast to turn and it kept going.

"Hopefully we lost them," said Ashley. "Let me

know where to turn to get back on the main road."

They passed a couple of small trailer homes on the side road. They all had plastic covering with old tires lined in a row along the tops of them to keep the indoor temperature stable.

"Up ahead here," said Jane. "If they kept going straight on the main road, we should be behind them now."

"Turn left here?" Ashley asked.

"Yes. Then turn right to go back onto the main road," said Jane.

Ashley made the turn and there was no sign of the truck. They traveled the final distance to the sacred mountain and turned onto a steep-looking single lane mountain road.

"How far up the mountain can we drive?" asked Ashley.

"It's hard to tell by the map," replied Jane. "This road isn't really marked on here. This is just at the mile marker where Jordan told us to turn. I guess we keep going as far as we can."

Peaches woke up and looked around. "Where are we?" she asked, rubbing her eyes. "Looks like nothing in every direction," Peaches observed.

"We're halfway up the sacred mountain," said Jane.

"It's a good thing we're in a Jeep," said Peaches. "This road looks gnarly. I wouldn't want to try to drive my car up this hill."

"Yup," said Ashley. "We've got this." She drove slowly over the bumps and large rocks and curves and climbed up the steep mountain road.

"I hope we're in the right place," said Jane. "It looks like we can't drive any farther, but there's a flat spot over there where you can park."

Ashley pulled over and parked the Jeep. "C'mon, Edward," she said, as she hooked on the leash. Edward leaped out of the Jeep with excitement and danced around the girls. He licked the girls' hands as they donned their small backpacks with water and snacks. They didn't know how far they would need to walk.

"Stop licking me," said Jane, as she wiped her hands on her shorts. Peaches wiped her hands off, too. Ashley pulled out a small container from under the seat and poured some water into it out of her water bottle and set it on the ground. Edward lapped it up until it was dry, and then walked over and peed on a large rock.

They all started climbing up the steep terrain over rocks and brush, almost to the top. They came to an opening in the side of the mountain with a fire pit in the front.

"Do you think this is it?" said Ashley.

"I hope so," said Jane. "We're almost at the top."

They slowly walked toward the opening. Jane called out. "Hello!"

They waited for a reply.

A small elderly woman dressed in buckskin, with long white hair in braids came out of the opening. Her skin was dark and wrinkled from the sun. Her small-framed body was bent from age, and her fingers looked crumpled from a life of hard work.

"Hello," said Jane. "Jordan sent us from the Yellowglen Tribal Museum."

"You come," said the woman, pointing at Jane. "You stay," she said, pointing to Ashley and Peaches.

Jane swallowed hard and gave a nervous look to Ashley and Peaches and mouthed, "Don't leave me." She followed her into the cave opening.

"Sit," said the woman, pointing to a stool cut from a log. Jane sat down.

"Who are you?" she asked.

"My name is Jane Teaberry."

"I am Hehewuti. What brings you here, Jane Teaberry?" she asked.

"I have some photos of some sand paintings, and I wondered if you could tell me what the symbols mean," said Jane. She pulled out her cell phone and showed her the photos. Jane took out a notebook and pen from her backpack to take notes.

"These look like they came from the Large Bear Tribe, who make sand paintings to sell," said the old woman, looking through the photos. "Sand paintings are destroyed after a sing. These are not sacred," she said.

"But someone created them for a reason. I'm trying to find out why these were created and why someone would steal them. Can you tell me what the symbols mean?" asked Jane.

She pointed with one of her crumpled looking fingers. "This symbol points to a place called Snake

Mountain. It is on private land. This symbol over here indicates fortune."

Jane scrolled to the other photo on her cell phone. The old woman pointed to the other photo. "This also shows Snake Mountain. These symbols here indicate battle with intruders. Spanish men likely. Brave warriors are buried there. This is sacred ground. Must be left alone. Evil spirits will punish those who trespass," said Hehewuti.

"Oh, wow," said Jane. "Is it far from here?"

"Not far. Don't go there. Sacred ground. Bad things can happen to you," said Hehewuti. "Your hair is dark, but your skin is pale. You do not live here. Why did you come to find this?" she asked Jane.

"Our friend was attacked and injured badly by someone who stole the original sand paintings from an Archaeology lab back in Ohio. I want to find out why and who did it," said Jane.

"The greedy ones," she nodded. "Always looking for treasure. You want to solve a mystery?" said the woman.

"I want to help solve it, so our friend, Carl, and my friend's dad will be safe," said Jane.

"You like helping," said the woman, nodding.

"Well, yes, I guess I do," said Jane.

The old woman reached out for Jane's hand. Jane held it out. The old woman took it in hers, and held Jane's palm out flat and pulled it towards her. She looked closely at it. "You like to solve mysteries. You try to be brave warrior, but you not so brave yet for yourself. You try to be brave for others. You will do important work in your life. You in danger now. Must be careful."

"In danger from what?" asked Jane.

"From who," said the woman. "Greedy people. Evil spirits. Must be careful. You go now. Stay safe."

Hehewuti pulled out a green stone from the small medicine bag around her neck. "Take this and keep it with you."

"Thank you," said Jane. "What kind of stone is this?"

"It will provide what you need, Jane Teaberry," said Hehewuti. "Keep it with you always."

"Thank you. Is there anything else you can tell me?" asked Jane.

"That's all. You go now," said Hehewuti.

"Thank you so much, Hehewuti," said Jane, as she got up to leave.

Jane emerged from the opening of the cave, and Edward wagged his whole body when he saw her. She gave him a quick pat on the head. "Let's go," she said.

"What's that?" asked Peaches.

"It's a stone that she gave me," said Jane.

"What does it do?" asked Ashley.

"It's supposed to be for protection or something. She didn't say exactly," said Jane.

"Did she give you any info?" asked Peaches.

"Yes, she said one of the symbols refers to a location called Snake Mountain."

"Ewww," said Peaches. "I hope there aren't any

snakes there."

"Why would they have named it Snake Mountain, if there weren't any snakes?" said Ashley. "At least it's not called Rattlesnake Mountain or Cobra Mountain."

"You're right about that," said Peaches.

The girls and Edward traversed carefully down the rocky path back to the Jeep. Jane was relieved that Peaches hadn't done something impulsive on the mountain top. There were no vines to save her this time.

Ashley maneuvered the Jeep and turned it around to head back down the mountain. They inched their way back to the main road and headed back toward the hotel.

"Check the map for Snake Mountain," said Ashley, as they were driving along.

"Got it, I'm looking," said Jane, with the paper map spread out in front of her. After a long look at the map, Jane couldn't find it.

"Nope, it's not on this map," reported Jane. She folded it up again and put it in the glove box.

It was past dinner time when they were finally near the hotel, so they stopped at a roadside diner to eat on the way back.

When they entered the hotel room, they were shocked to find it had been ransacked. They asked the hotel manager to call the local sheriff to report it. A deputy came out to write a report.

"Is anything missing?" asked Deputy Dave

Robbins.

"Not that we can tell," said Jane. "I don't think so."

"Do you have any idea who would want to look through your stuff? Or do you have something you know someone else wants?" he asked.

"Not really," said Jane. "Just our clothes are here. And my friend, Peaches, has a nice camera, but she had it with her. We had some photos back in Ohio that someone stole from us in a restaurant, but we don't have them here, except on my cell phone."

"Who stole them?" he asked.

"I don't know who or why. I just know it was a man with brownish hair wearing jeans and a blue shirt," said Jane.

"Where were you before you came back to the hotel?" asked Deputy Dave.

"We visited a woman called Hehewuti up on the sacred mountain today and she said to be careful because we are in danger from greedy evil people. She didn't tell me who they were or what they wanted."

"You went to the sacred mountain to see Hehewuti?" asked the deputy with a surprised look on his face.

"Yes," said Jane. "Why?"

"She doesn't usually let outsiders come there. She's very choosy about who she'll talk to," he said.

"We were sent there by Jordan from the Yellowglen Tribal Museum, but I don't know how she would have known we were coming. She's completely isolated up there. But she did only let me in," said

Jane.

"That was lucky that she was willing, since you're not from any local tribes," said the deputy.

"I guess it was," replied Jane.

"Well, I'll file this report. I don't know how we'll find out who did this. There are no surveillance cameras here. Just be careful, especially if Hehewuti told you that you were in danger. She's never wrong about anything," said the deputy.

"Okay, then," said Ashley. "That's not what I would call reassuring."

"It's all I have," said the deputy. "I'll do what I can."

"Thanks," said Ashley.

After the deputy left, the girls sat down together to talk about what Hehewuti told Jane.

"So, if I'm understanding correctly," said Ashley, "we have Snake Mountain on both paintings. Then one of them has an indication of fortune, and the other one has a battle between a tribe and some Spanish men. Warriors are buried there, and it's sacred ground and we shouldn't go there because something bad might happen."

"Yep, that's pretty much what she said," said Jane.

"I guess we need to find Snake Mountain," said Peaches, "but hopefully not the snakes or the evil spirits."

"I guess we do," agreed Ashley.

CHAPTER TEN

SARAH LIGHTFOOT EMMONS

THE NEXT MORNING, Peaches called her dad to let him know how things were going.

"I don't want you to stay at the hotel another night," said Dr. Parker firmly. "I'll arrange for a safer place for you to stay. I'll call Sarah Lightfoot Emmons, the woman who let us set up the excavation on her property this summer. She's a nice lady, and I don't think it'll be a problem. I'll call you right back."

A few minutes later, Dr. Parker called Peaches back. "Sarah said she'd be happy to have you girls as guests at her house. It's in Chupacabra County. I'll text you the address. Go ahead and go there now. I want you out of the hotel ASAP."

"Okay, Dad. Thanks!" said Peaches.

The girls and Edward checked out of the hotel and headed to Sarah's house, which was a long drive from where they had been staying. "So much driving!" said Ashley. "I'm glad we're finally here. At least I hope we are."

She drove the Jeep down a long driveway to an area where there was a black pickup truck and a red two-door Jeep with a bikini top parked in front of a large garage.

The old adobe and stone house had fresh coat of mud plaster and looked well maintained. There was a porch that wrapped around the two sides of the house that were in view. Small bundles of red chili peppers hung from the porch overhang to dry. The large structure almost looked lonely against the flat landscape surrounding it.

"Does this look like the right place?" asked Jane. "We're clearly not anywhere near Ohio. That's for sure." Jane had never been to this part of the country and it looked different from anywhere she'd ever been.

"I don't know. It's the address my dad gave me, so I guess it's right," replied Peaches.

Aside from the few juniper trees in the yard that looked like they were planted there to accent the house, there were mostly small clumps of green shrubs that scattered themselves across the desert land, allowing a majestic view of the mountains that loomed across the background.

"Do we have this much sky at home?" asked Peaches. She pulled out her camera while the Jeep was still moving.

Jane laughed. "I guess we just can't see it very well because we have so many trees back home."

"These pics are gonna be great," said Peaches,

snapping photos in every direction.

Edward hopped out of the Jeep first as soon as Ashley opened the door. "Stop. Edward!" said Ashley. Edward immediately put on the brakes and turned his head to look at Ashley. A small cloud of dust erupted underneath him where he stopped. "If you have to pee, go ahead. Just don't run off," she said. He trotted over to the nearest shrub to pee. Ashley grabbed his bowl from under the seat and poured some water in it. Edward lapped it up and then sat down to wait for instructions.

Jane and Peaches had started walking toward the house, and Ashley and Edward followed.

Sarah, who is in her sixties, was already waiting on the porch when they had pulled up to her house. She wore her long white hair pulled back into a large braid and wore a long skirt and sandals. She walked elegantly down the front steps to greet them. "Welcome ladies," she said with a warm smile.

"I'm Peaches, and this is Ashley and Jane and Edward. I hope my dad told you we have a dog with us," said Peaches. "Is that alright, Ms. Emmons?"

"Oh, yes. Call me Sarah," said Sarah. She reached over to pat Edward on the head. He wagged his tail and tried to lick her hand.

"Come on in, and I'll show you where you'll be staying." They followed her inside.

"Two of you can stay in this room, and then one of you can have this other room," said Sarah.

"You two can stay together," said Ashley, "and Edward and I will take the single room."

"Sounds good," said Jane. The girls dropped their backpacks in their rooms and followed Sarah out to the large open kitchen.

Jane looked around at the colorful kitchen cabinets and Mexican tile backsplash over the sink. French doors led to a large tile patio surrounded by a garden in the back of the house, and extended the magnificent view from the large picture window across the back wall of the house. "I love all the beautiful colors in your kitchen," she said. "And your garden is gorgeous."

"Thank you, Jane. Please, have a seat. Would you girls like some lemonade or tea?" said Sarah.

"Lemonade sounds great," said Peaches. "I'm parched."

"Lemonade sounds good to me," agreed Ashley.

They sat down at the table with Sarah to drink their lemonade. "You have a beautiful home," said Jane. "Thank you for letting us stay with you."

"You're welcome," said Sarah, with a smile. "It gets kind of lonely out here, so I'm happy to have the company. So, you're Dr. Parker's gorgeous daughter?" she asked Peaches.

"Yes, I guess that's me," said Peaches, looking down at the floor and shrugging her shoulders.

"He talked a lot about you when he was here. He's a nice man, and he really knows Archaeology. I grew up here, and then inherited this estate from my family, and there had been some indications that there may have been an ancient village here at one time. I wanted someone I could trust to check into it. I'm so glad he brought the students out here to do some excavating. It all went very well."

"You can definitely trust my dad," said Peaches.

"I feel like I can. So, what brings you girls all the way to New Mexico?" asked Sarah.

"We're trying to research the sand paintings that Dr. Parker found in the cave when he was here," said Jane. "There isn't enough information about them that we could look up from home."

"Oh, I do remember those," said Sarah. "That was an interesting find. When I was a child, I used to find pieces of pottery, stone tools, animal bones, and arrowheads in the yard. Sometimes a piece of pottery was just sticking up out of the earth. I love learning about history, and it was fascinating to me, so I started collecting the pieces that I found. But once I was an adult, and then inherited the property, I thought it was time to find out what else was underneath here. I so hoped there were more signs of a village. Someone was definitely here before we were and I would love to know more about them."

"That's really neat," said Jane. "I would have loved to have found stuff like that in the yard when I was a kid."

"I didn't want anyone digging here for profit," said Sarah. "Dr. Parker assured me that his students would act professionally and after they assessed the items that they found, they would return them or deliver them to a museum, or whatever I wanted to do. They were here for the experience and knowledge.

That was exactly what I had wanted."

Just then a sandy-haired man came in the back door and entered the kitchen. He looked to be in his mid-thirties, wearing a white t-shirt, jeans, boots, a cowboy hat, and work gloves. Jane thought he looked as though he had spent a lot of time in the sun.

"This is my houseman, Andy. Andy, this is Jane, Ashley, Peaches, and Edward. If there is anything you need while you're here, just ask Andy."

"Nice to meet you all," said Andy, tipping his hat.

"Nice to meet you," said the girls.

"If you'd like to go horseback riding while you're here, I have a stable with some horses," said Sarah. "Dakota can help you with that. He takes good care of them. You may also see him or his wife, Kaydee, around the property, but mostly they stay near the stable. They live in a cottage next to it."

"That sounds fun!" said Peaches.

"Come let me show you some of the items that I found," she said, as she arose from the table. "Follow me."

They followed her through a pair of carved wooden doors into another room that had a large stone fireplace. The opening to the fireplace was almost as tall as Jane. The large grate stood empty, and the smooth brick in the firewalls looked clean, as though it had not been used recently. The large stones that decorated the front looked like they had been carefully collected and placed with a keen eye.

Jane noticed the wooden beams that were in

rows across the ceiling. There was a large skylight that allowed in a good amount of sunlight and brightened up the room. The furniture was mostly covered in leather, and a traditional looking Indian blanket was draped over an upholstered chair in the corner. An area rug with a Southwestern design lay across the center of the tile floor.

On the wall next to the fireplace, there were three large display cases full of pottery, arrowheads, some stone tools and some items that Jane couldn't quite identify. "You found all these items near the top of the ground?" said Jane.

"Over my lifetime," said Sarah. "I spent a lot of time outdoors here as a child."

"That's amazing," said Peaches.

"Let's go outside and I'll show you the dig area, where the students were working," said Sarah. The girls and Edward followed her outside and they walked about a half mile towards the East side of the property.

Most of the land near the house was flat, but there were hills behind the house and near the dig. The hills became much more elevated as Jane looked towards the mountainous area farther behind the house.

"How much land do you own?" asked Ashley, looking around at acres of nothing. "Is it okay to ask that?"

"Yes, it's fine. About 600 acres," said Sarah. "It extends all the way up those hills," she said, as she pointed towards them. "I haven't even seen some of it. It gets pretty mountainous. But the excavation area isn't too far from the house."

They kept walking until they saw the excavation area. It started to get a little more hilly as they got closer to it. There were rectangular sections that were carefully roped off with stakes at the corners, and each rectangle was covered by a blue tarp. There were a couple of tents set up nearby.

"I'm leaving this as is, until we decide what to do next," said Sarah. "Dr. Parker may come back for another session with his students. I'm not sure yet."

Jane looked around trying to locate the cave where the sand paintings were found. "Is that a cave over there?" she asked.

"I guess you could call it a cave. There is an opening there, but it's small. I'm not sure what is in there and I don't know if it's safe to explore. Dr. Parker kept the students out of it. He did step in with a flashlight and found some items near the entrance."

"It's beautiful out here," said Peaches. "I've never seen anyplace like it." She kept her camera hanging around her neck and took a lot of photos.

"Yes, it is," said Sarah. She looked at her watch. "I need to run to the market. Andy is in the house if you need anything. You're free to wander around the grounds if you like. Will you be here for dinner at 6:30?"

"That sounds great," said Jane. "Thank you. We'll be there."

"Great, I'll see you girls later," said Sarah. She headed back to the house.

Ashley took Edward off his leash to let him run around a bit. Edward sniffed around the tarps, and stayed close by.

"Yeah, Edward, what is under those tarps?" said Peaches. After Sarah was out of sight, Peaches went over to one of the tarps and moved the cement blocks on one corner and lifted it up to take a look. "I just want to see what's in here," she said. "Nothing but dirt!" She covered it back up.

"That must be the cave where your dad found the sand paintings," observed Jane, pointing to the small opening.

"If it's a cave, it doesn't look very big," said Ashley.

Peaches headed over to the opening and disappeared.

"Did she just go into the cave?" asked Ashley.

"She must have," said Jane.

They walked over to the cave entrance. "Peaches, are you in there?" yelled Jane.

"In here," called Peaches.

Edward darted into the cave when he heard Peaches' voice. "Come out of there," called Jane.

"Edward!" called Ashley. Neither one of them came out. Ashley stepped inside the cave. "Edward!" she called.

No one came out. Jane sighed. She followed them all inside. "Where are you?" said Jane. "Please come out."

CHAPTER ELEVEN
TRAPPED!

"EDWARD! PEACHES! Where are you?" said Ashley.

"Over here," said Peaches. "I seem to have stepped into a hole."

Ashley used the flashlight app on her cell phone to look around. She spotted Peaches and Edward. "Over here, Jane," said Ashley. "Follow my flashlight beam."

The cave was cold and damp inside. "Yuk," Jane said to herself, as she squinted her eyes to see in the dark. It was so dark she could barely see her hand in front of her face with the limited light coming in from the entrance and Ashley's flashlight. She had to step carefully, because the bottom was a combination of sticky mud and slippery rock and she wasn't sure what was right in front of her.

Jane couldn't help feeling annoyed and frustrated that Peaches had put them in this situation.

She loved that Peaches was adventurous, but Jane never knew what her friend might do on an impulse.

Jane found her way over to Peaches and Ashley. Ashley shined her light on Peaches' leg. Jane could only see her leg part of the way below her knee.

"Wow, you're really stuck," observed Jane.

"No kidding," said Peaches flatly. "How 'bout gettin' me outta here?"

"We're gonna have to do some digging," said Ashley. "See if you can find anything to use for a shovel, Jane."

Jane used her cell phone flashlight to look around for a shovel. She found a few bones and then a small shovel with a broken handle. "I found an old broken shovel!" said Jane. "Talk about luck."

What was left of the handle was only a few inches long and the head of the shovel looked old and fragile. Jane kneeled down and started gently digging away from Peaches' leg with the old shovel, while Ashley held the light on her. As she moved dirt away from Peaches' leg, more of it was falling in on her.

"I can't dig fast enough." Jane was getting frustrated at her lack of progress.

"You need to try to pull your leg out as much as you can while Jane digs," said Ashley.

"Okay," said Peaches.

Jane then tried working on the opposite side, and slowly was able to move enough dirt for Peaches to pull her foot out.

"Free at last!" said Peaches. She grabbed her ankle. "But ouch, it hurts."

"It's probably bruised from that rock beside the hole," said Ashley. "Try not to put much weight on it." Peaches sat down on a large rock formation and rubbed her ankle. Jane sat down on a flat rock near the floor of the cave and breathed a sigh of relief. "Finally!" she said. Edward came over to sit beside her and licked her face. Jane laughed. "Thanks, Edward."

Ashley shined her light around the cave to see what was in there. She spotted a wooden handle and went over to see what it was. It looked like an old pick tool. There was a bucket next to it. "I wonder why these are here," she said. "Someone must have been digging in here a long time ago."

"I wonder why there are bones in here," said Jane. "I saw several large bones and it's creeping me out. Can we get out of here now?"

"Def," said Ashley. "Let's grab Peaches and go."

Just then there was a large rumbling noise and the cave started shaking. Rocks started raining down on them. "Cover your heads!" yelled Ashley.

They all ducked and covered their heads. Ashley threw herself on top of Edward to protect him. When the rumbling stopped, the small beam of light from the opening disappeared. "I can't even see my hand in front of my face," said Jane. "Every bit of light is gone."

"Okay, which way is the opening?" asked Ashley. "Go find the opening, Edward."

Edward wagged his tail and spun around,

sniffing the walls of the cave. He seemed confused. He trotted back over to Ashley, sniffed her hand, and sat down.

"Um, Edward is sitting beside me," said Ashley, knowing that no one could see him. "He seems to have given up."

"That's not a good sign," said Peaches. "I don't want to die! I'm so sorry for coming in here. I didn't know we'd have to die here."

"Maybe we shouldn't have come on this trip at all. Me and my bright ideas," said Jane.

"You two get a grip on yourselves. Are you going to let a little rock slide get the best of us?" said Ashley. "Just sit tight and Edward and I will see if we can find a way out."

Jane turned on her flashlight app on her cell phone to see if she could find where the opening used to be. She shined it around the area where she was standing until she saw a skeleton in the corner. "Um, there's a skeleton over there."

"Where?" asked Peaches.

"That way," said Jane. She shined her light on it.

"O M G," said Peaches. "We're in here with the dead."

"So... the dead can't hurt us... or help us get out of here. You two stay here, and Edward and I are going to head that way, and see if we can find another way out," said Ashley." Ashley and Edward started walking in the opposite direction from the opening where they entered the cave.

"Peaches needs to stay put anyway, but I'm

going to go back the way we came in to look around," said Jane. "You keep an eye on the skeleton, Peaches."

"Very funny, Jane," said Peaches. "I'm going to call my dad, because I don't know Sarah's number."

Peaches pulled out her cell phone and tried to call. "No reception in here," she said, shoving her cell phone back into her pocket in a huff.

Jane started looking around in the direction that they came in. She spotted an old piece of paper on the ground and folded it and put it in her pocket. She kept the light on the ground in front of her so she wouldn't step into a hole like Peaches did. She found what she thought was the opening where they entered, but it was completely covered. She turned around and found her way back to where Peaches was waiting.

"I think I found the entrance and it's completely covered," said Jane as she stepped carefully back towards Peaches. "We're going to have to find another way out."

"I hope there is one," said Peaches.

Jane stopped when she got close to where she started, and shined her light around at the glistening walls. She spotted a narrow opening. "I wonder if that's a way out," she said.

"Just stay here," said Peaches.

"I can't just do nothing," said Jane. "I promise I won't go far."

"Okay, but be careful," said Peaches.

Jane carefully stepped through the sticky mud over to the opening. It was about three feet wide and five feet high at first. She squatted down, so that her head would not brush the ceiling, and she inched her way several feet into the passageway, keeping her light shining all around to see what was there. She tried not to touch the walls, not knowing what might be crawling around on them.

The passageway seemed to get more and more narrow and the floor sloped progressively downward. It seemed to be just a long and winding tunnel and Jane became more nervous as she inched farther into it. Her heart was beating wildly, as she wondered if there were snakes or bats ahead or if she would suddenly drop into a deep black hole.

Jane was just about to turn back, when the passageway opened into a large circular room with a small pond in the middle of it. Her heart pounded as she tried to decide what to do. She stopped at the end of the tunnel and shined her light around the room.

Jane took a deep breath and then stepped out into the room and walked over to the pond and shone her light into it. She saw some tiny eyeless fish swimming around. She stopped and gazed up at the ceiling looking for bats. She wasn't sure if there were any up there, but she did see a number of stalactites hanging down. Some were dripping small drops of water into the pond. She turned all the way around the room with her light.

She saw no other way out of the room. There were some moderately sized stalagmite formations on the cave floor near the wall that she used to try to scrape off some of the mud that had caked onto her shoes. Not much of it came off.

Jane suddenly felt nervous about the possibility of being trapped in the room, and decided to go back. She ducked down and slipped into the passageway, squatted again to step through, but moved a little faster than before. She found her way back into the main room. She felt relieved when she stepped back out of the passageway, even though it was so dark that she couldn't see if she was in the same place where she had started.

"Peaches?" she called, praying there would be an answer.

"Still right here," said Peaches.

Jane made her way over and sat down on the rock next to her. "How's your ankle?" she asked.

"Still hurts. What did you find?" she asked.

"Not much, just another room that doesn't go anywhere."

"I hope Ashley isn't lost," said Peaches. "It's been a while."

"Me, too," said Jane. "I guess we'll just have to wait. It's super dark in here, but I'm going to leave my flashlight off to save my phone battery."

"It's creepy, sitting here in the dark, knowing that skeleton is over there in the corner," said Peaches.

"Yeah, I wonder why that person was here and what happened," said Jane.

"I'm going to try not to think about what happened," said Peaches. "I don't want the same thing to happen to us. Who knows what else is in here with us. Probably bats and snakes."

"I'm going to ignore that," said Jane. She had wondered the same thing but wasn't going to say it out loud.

Time passed and the girls started getting colder. "Brrr, I'm freezing. It's really damp in here," said Jane.

"We're doomed," said Peaches. "I think we've been here for over an hour, probably two hours, and no sign of Ashley and Edward."

"We're not doomed!" said Jane. "Don't say that!"

"But we are," said Peaches. "Just like the skeleton."

"We haven't been here that long," said Jane.

"Maybe we should try again to find another way out," said Peaches. "I don't want to just sit here until we die. We need to do something to help ourselves."

"Yeah, you're right," said Jane. "I don't want someone coming in here 20 years from now saying, 'there are those two girls who didn't try hard enough to find a way out.'"

"Yeah," said Peaches, nodding in agreement. "I don't either."

"I could try going in the direction that Ashley went."

"That makes sense, since it's the only other direction you haven't tried," said Peaches.

"Can you walk yet?" asked Jane.

"My ankle does feel a little better, but I think I'd slow you down," said Peaches. "If... I mean... when... you find an opening you can come back and get me."

Jane stood up and looked at her cell phone. "I still have some battery left." She turned on the flashlight on her phone and shined it toward the back of the cave where Ashley and Edward had gone. "Wait, listen. Do you hear barking?"

"Mmm, maybe... YES! I do hear barking!" said Peaches.

The barking got louder and then they saw some lights. "Over here!" called Jane. "We're right here."

"Not so loud," said Peaches. "Rocks might start falling again."

Suddenly, Edward came bounding towards them with lights following him. "Hey, Edward, here boy," Jane whispered. He snuggled up to Jane and licked her face when she bent towards him to give him a hug.

"Where's your person?" Jane asked. "Where's Ash?" He wagged his tail and barked once.

"Shhh," said Peaches. "Bark quietly."

Ashley appeared right behind him. "Good boy, Edward!" she said. "You found them."

"We thought you were gone forever, swallowed up in the cave," said Peaches.

"Nope, not today," said Ashley.

They heard some men's voices and then Andy appeared with another man. Both men were carrying flashlights.

"Edward and I found a small opening, but I was afraid if I came back to get you first, we might not find it again. So, we climbed out and I got some help."

"You girls okay?" said Andy.

"We're freezing, but we're okay," said Jane. "Thanks so much for coming to help us!"

"Yes, thank you!" said Peaches. "We thought we were doomed."

"You thought we were," said Jane.

"Whatever," said Peaches. "I'm just glad we're not."

"This is Dakota. He runs the stable. Let's get you girls out of here," said Andy. "Follow us."

Edward barked and wagged his tail. Jane helped Peaches get up from the rock where she was sitting. Peaches hung her arm around Jane's shoulder and she limped along behind Andy and Dakota. Ashley and Edward stayed behind them to make sure no one got lost.

They walked a long way. "This is a big cave," said Jane. "Much bigger than I imagined."

"Yeah, no kidding," said Ashley. "Edward and I walked a long way in the dark, not knowing if we were going deeper underground or whether we were getting closer to an opening. Luckily, we found a way out."

They soon arrived at the opening. Andy and Dakota had made it larger and stabilized it before they came into the cave to find Jane and Peaches.

Jane could see the light shining in from outside into the cave. She was immediately relieved, and could feel her entire body relax all of a sudden. Her breathing slowed down to normal. She didn't realize how tense she had been until now.

Andy climbed out first. Then the others pushed Peaches out, while Andy grabbed her by the hand and pulled her. Then Jane. Then Edward. Then Ashley. Then Dakota.

Jane breathed a sigh of relief when they were all out of the cave. The sun was starting to set, making her aware that they had spent hours trapped in the cave.

"Thanks for your help, Dakota," said Andy.

"You're welcome," said Dakota. "I'm glad you ladies are okay. I'll head back to the stable if you don't need anything else."

"We're good," said Andy. Dakota tipped his cowboy hat, and mounted a horse that was tied to a tree and rode off to the stable.

"Girls, we need to get back to the house. Sarah has dinner waiting for you. The rest of us are going to have to walk though."

It was beginning to get dark as they walked with Andy to the house. Jane could hear several animals howling in the distance.

"What is that?" she asked.

"Just some coyotes," said Andy. "Nothing to worry about. If you see one, just make some noise and they should leave you alone. People will tell you to bang some pots and pans, but I don't usually carry any with me." He laughed.

"Good to know," said Jane.

Sarah was waiting at the door for them. "I'm so relieved you girls are okay," she said as she hugged each of them. "I didn't know what to think when you didn't return for dinner. I'm so glad Ashley came back to the house to get Andy to come help."

"We're sorry to have worried you," said Jane. "Thanks for holding supper for us."

"I didn't think that cave was safe," said Sarah. "Dr. Parker didn't let any of the students go in there. He found a couple of items right inside the small opening, but was reluctant to go any further without some investigation."

"He's not going to be happy to find out it's my fault we were trapped in there. I went in there first and they came in to find me," said Peaches.

"Well, you're all safe now," said Sarah. "Thanks for your help, Andy."

"I'm glad it turned out well," said Andy. "I'll see you all in the morning."

"G'night, Andy. Thanks," said the girls in unison.

"Please, girls, sit down and have something to eat. You must be hungry after that ordeal. You probably haven't eaten anything since lunch," said Sarah.

Jane looked at the delicious-looking spread of food in the center of the table. There were burritos, enchiladas, and some chiles rellenos, made from green chiles stuffed with lots of Jack cheese, along with large bowl of blue corn tortilla chips and salsa.

Jane felt bad that Sarah had to keep everything warm for them. "I'm so sorry we were so late getting back here. This looks wonderful!"

"I'm starving," said Ashley. "This looks great!"

"Thanks, Sarah," said Peaches, as she sat down at the table. "We will clean this up when we finish eating. You've done so much work preparing this for us."

"I'm happy to have you girls here and I enjoy cooking. Really, it's no trouble," she said, as she sat down with them to enjoy the meal.

Sarah started serving her plate. "Tell me about this cave you explored today."

Peaches started telling the story, as they filled Sarah in on what the cave was like inside and enjoyed their meal together. They enjoyed natillas for dessert, which is a custard topped with cinnamon.

"Best meal ever!" said Ashley.

CHAPTER TWELVE
ASHLEY'S CONFESSION

"GOOD MORNING, LADIES," said Sarah, as she peeked her head in the bedroom door where Jane had just awakened.

"Good morning," said Jane. Peaches was still asleep.

"I just wanted to let you girls know that I set out some breakfast goodies for you in the kitchen. I'm going out for a while and will be back later. Andy is here if you need anything," said Sarah.

"Thanks so much," said Jane. "We all really appreciate it."

"I'll see you later today," said Sarah, as she closed the bedroom door.

Jane got up and wandered into the kitchen. She brushed her long, dark hair out of her face and sat down at the table, trying to wake up. Edward heard her in the kitchen and followed her from the next room. Jane could hear his toenails clicking on the tile floor and she smiled.

"Good morning, boy," said Jane. "Let's see what Sarah left us to eat." Edward wagged his tail and sniffed the air.

"I'm sure Ash has something tasty for you, too," said Jane.

Ashley shuffled into the room in her pajamas, yawning. "I wondered where he went."

"He's fine," said Jane. "Not causing any trouble."

Ashley plopped down in a chair at the kitchen table. "He doesn't usually," said Ashley. "But I had to make sure."

"Sarah left us some breakfast. Help yourself," said Jane, pointing to the food.

"Looks fab!" said Ashley, as she picked up a jelly doughnut. "I'm going for the doughnuts first."

"I hardly know where to begin," said Jane. "Yogurt, fruit, doughnuts, eggs, bacon. She sure knows how to feed people," said Jane.

"She sure does," said Ashley. "So, what are we doing today?"

"I want to go look at the cave opening and find out if it closed up by itself or if someone closed us in there," said Jane.

"You think someone tried to trap us?" asked Ashley.

"Maybe," said Jane. "I want to know for sure."

"Well, I do, too," said Ashley. "I wasn't thinking that was the case, but we need to know if someone did."

"Should we go now and let Peaches sleep, or should I wake her up?" said Jane.

"I say wake her up," said Ashley. "She'll get over it."

"Okay, I'll go get her."

Jane came back out of the bedroom with a sleepy Peaches. "Here's breakfast," said Jane. "Help yourself."

"Thanks," said Peaches. She yawned and slid down into a chair at the table, trying to open her eyes.

"I've been trying to decide whether to tell you this," said Ashley, "because you might think I'm crazy." She hesitated for a moment.

Jane and Peaches turned to look at Ashley with their eyes wide open. "Spill it, sister," said Peaches.

"Well... er... when Edward and I were searching for a way out of the cave, we saw some light. As we approached, I saw some people sitting around a campfire."

"A campfire in the cave?" asked Jane.

"That's what it looked like at first, but then Edward ran right through the middle of it. It wasn't really there. It was like a hologram or something."

"Wha?" said Peaches.

"Who were the people?" asked Jane.

"They looked like American Indians. At least that was how they were dressed. Maybe three of them. The women were dressed in buckskin. It looked like they were cooking something. There was a man with long braids and he wasn't wearing a shirt. They didn't look up when we approached, or when Edward ran through their fire."

"Weird," said Peaches. "They must have been spirits, maybe ghosts. My dad has seen some ghosty people like that around some of his digs."

"Really?" said Jane. "That's interesting."

"Or it's possible you are crazy and you hallucinated them." Peaches laughed.

"I started to walk around them," said Ashley, "when I saw a man standing behind them. He also looked like an American Indian. He motioned to me to follow him, so I did. When we got past the campfire people, it was dark again, but I could still see him. There was a glow of some sort around him. Edward and I followed him for a bit and then he showed us the spot where some sunlight was peeking into the cave. He stood beside it and pointed to it. That's how we found a way out. As soon as I saw it, the man disappeared."

"Well, that's cool," said Peaches. "We should thank him if we see him." She chuckled. "Really. He probably saved our lives."

"I agree," said Jane. "I didn't think we were getting out of there."

"I was sure we were going to die," said Peaches.

"I know you were," said Jane, nodding.

"We're going back to check out the opening of the cave to see why it got covered up after breakfast. We'll thank him if he shows up again," said Ashley. "How's your ankle?"

"It's okay, I guess," said Peaches. "After I put

ice on it last night, it felt better. I can walk on it now."
She looked at the breakfast spread. "Is there coffee?"

"Yes, here you go," said Jane. She poured coffee into a mug for Peaches.

"Thanks," said Peaches. She set the mug down on the table in front of her.

"Are you going to drink that like it is?" asked Jane.

"Of course not. Where's the sugar and cream? Is there any caramel syrup?" asked Peaches with a smile.

"No caramel, but we have cream and sugar," said Jane.

"That'll have to do." Peaches laughed.

"Do you think you can walk all the way back to the cave?"

"I think so," said Peaches.

"Great. I'll meet you out on the front porch when everyone is dressed and ready to go," said Jane. She started heading toward the bedroom.

"Got it," said Ashley.

After everyone ate and got dressed, they started out to the excavation site to check what used to be the cave opening.

When they reached the site, they couldn't believe their eyes. Every tarp was pulled back and several of the rectangular sections looked like someone had been digging.

"I wonder who did this," said Jane.

"Let's check the cave entrance," said Ashley. They walked over to where the opening had been.

"So, what do you think?" said Jane. "Was it a natural occurrence, or did someone do it?"

"It looks like rocks rolled down from the hill," said Peaches, "and piled up here at the bottom. The opening wasn't very big when it was an opening."

"I can't tell if it happened on purpose," said Ashley. "I guess someone could have gone up the hill and caused a rockslide, either on purpose or accidentally."

"Yeah, I don't know how to tell either," said Jane. "But someone purposely was digging in the excavation site. I doubt they had permission because of the way they left it – uncovered and all. I doubt Sarah would be okay with that."

Peaches put her hands on her hips. "So, what you're saying is that, coincidentally, the cave opening got blocked at the same time that someone was messing around the dig site and you're not sure if it's related?" said Peaches. "Um, what do you think happened?"

"We need to let Sarah know, or Andy, unless he had something to do with it," said Ashley.

"Do you think he would have done it?" said Jane.

"I dunno," said Ashley. "We don't really know him."

"I guess that's true," said Jane. "Let's head back to the house."

As they walked back to the house, Ashley suddenly exclaimed, "I almost forgot to tell you!"

She pulled three gold coins out of her pocket.

"When Edward and I were searching the cave for a way out, I found these coins in a bucket next to another skeleton."

"Another skeleton?" said Peaches. "Ewww!"

"Let me see," said Jane. "Wow, they look old. I wonder how they ended up in the cave."

"They were in the bucket," said Ashley. "So, they must have something to do with why the skeleton people were in there digging."

"Hmmm," said Jane. "That makes sense."

"Let's go back to that center and ask Jordan if he knows anything about the coins," said Peaches.

"Good idea!" said Ashley.

When they got back to the house, the girls and Edward all got into Ashley's Jeep.

"Wait a sec," said Peaches, spotting Andy's red Jeep in the driveway.

"What?" asked Jane.

"I want to leave a duck for Andy," said Peaches.

Ashley smiled. "Yeah!" She pulled an open bag of small rubber ducks out of the glove box. "Pick one," she said.

"I like this green dragon one," said Peaches, grabbing the duck out of the bag. She looked around to make sure Andy wasn't around, then hopped out of the Jeep and shoved the duck onto Andy's door handle. She ran back to Ashley's Jeep and hopped back in.

"Ready," said Peaches. Ashley pulled out and headed back to the Yellowglen Tribal Museum.

"Is Jordan available?" asked Jane, when they reached the information desk.

"I can check," said the girl behind the desk.

"Tell him it's Jane Teaberry, and it's important," said Jane.

"Okay," said the girl. She left for about ten minutes and came back with Jordan.

"Hello again," he said. "Did you have any trouble finding Hehewuti?"

"No, we found her and she was willing to talk to us. Thank you," said Jane.

"Well, what did she say?" said Jordan.

"She said the paintings pointed to Snake Mountain, but we haven't found out where that is yet," said Jane.

"Oh, I can point you to it," said Jordan. "Come over to my computer." They followed him around past the information desk and to an office. He pulled up a map on his computer.

"It's not far from here, maybe 50 miles at the most. It's in Chupacabra County. You go down this road here, and then through this small town. Then you turn this way, here, see. Then you'll reach the Emmons estate. Snake Mountain is on this part of the estate. But it's private land. I don't know if they'll let you go there. But what did Hehewuti say about it?"

"She said don't go there," said Peaches. "Right, Jane?"

"Yes, pretty much. She said there was a battle there with the Spanish men and that warriors were killed there and it was sacred ground and don't go there."

"Ah, yes. You have to beware of sacred ground because bad things can happen to you if you disturb it."

"The funny thing is, that we were just near there this morning and didn't know we were so close to Snake Mountain.," said Jane, as she cut her eyes over to look at Peaches and Ashley. She wasn't sure who she could trust at this point, and was hoping they wouldn't say anything.

"The reason we came today is because Ash found some gold coins ... um... where we were hiking yesterday. Show him, Ash."

Ashley pulled out the coins. "Do you know what these are?"

Jordan looked closely at the coins. "These look Spanish," he said. "Where were they?"

"Where we were hiking yesterday," said Jane, wondering if she should trust giving him any more information.

"There are a lot of stories of Spanish gold being buried in different places around here, but no one knows if any of the stories are true," said Jordan. "If you want to leave them with me, I can do some research."

"I appreciate it," said Jane. "But they don't actually belong to us. We need to return them. But thanks for all of your help!"

"Okay, then," said Jordan, looking confused. "Let me know if you find out anything."

"We will," said Jane. "We have to get back now,

though. Oh, wait. I wanted to ask you about something else."

"What is it?" asked Jordan.

"Hehewuti gave me a stone and told me to always keep it with me. Do you know what this is?" asked Jane. She pulled it out of her pocket and held it out for Jordan to see.

He picked it up out of her hand. "Hmmm," he said. "I think I know but I want to verify." He pulled out a chart from his desk drawer. "It's aventurine," he said.

"Is that like something that will help her have good adventures?" asked Peaches.

"No, not exactly," said Jordan. "Aventurine is supposed to help her release fears and anxiety and replace it with confidence and leadership. It will help her increase her internal power."

Jordan handed the stone back to Jane. "It sounds like a good stone to have," he said.

Jane looked surprised. "Oh. That sounds like a really good thing. I'll make sure to keep it with me. Thanks, Jordan."

The girls left the center and headed back to the Jeep. "I hope we didn't share too much with him," said Jane. "I suddenly realized that our hotel room was trashed right after we spoke to him last time."

"Oh, that's right!" said Peaches. "But I don't think we shared too much. He doesn't know where we're staying now."

"Let's get back to Sarah's house," said Ashley, as she shut her door and started the engine. "More driving. Keep an eye out to make sure no one is following us."

"Will do," said Peaches. She turned slightly so she could watch out the back. Edward laid down beside her in the backseat and put his head into her lap.

CHAPTER THIRTEEN
GHOST TOWN

"THIS TWO-LANE ROAD is getting boring," said Ashley, after they had driven for a while. "Check the map and see how much farther to Sarah's house."

Jane unfolded the map. "Sorry, Ash. We still have 20 miles to go," she said.

"Ugh, I need a break. Let's stop at the next town," said Ashley.

"There's a town up ahead called Los Caballos Perdidos," said Jane. "That work?"

"I guess," said Ashley. "Let me know when we're close."

"Gotcha," said Jane. "I could use some ice cream."

"That sounds good to me," said Peaches, from the back seat. "That's a long name for a town. I'm gonna look it up and see what it means."

Peaches pulled out her phone and started pressing keys. "Found it!" she announced.

"What does it mean?" asked Jane.

"The Lost Horses," said Peaches.

"Interesting," said Jane. "There must be a story behind that. Maybe we'll find out what it is."

"It might be full of horses, because that's where the lost horses went, or there might be no horses, because they all got lost," said Peaches.

"That makes sense," said Ashley.

"It says here that it was a thriving town back in the 1600s. It was a cultural trade center, but there were conflicts with the Spanish, and heavy drought and famine that weakened the town," said Peaches.

"Then I wonder if it's still there. It looks like three more miles. We'll find out soon," said Jane. "It's on the left."

"Got it," said Ashley. They drove a few more miles until Jane spotted a small sign hanging on an old rusty chain beside a dirt road.

"This might be it," said Jane.

"The sign looks really old," said Peaches. "It looks like it says 'Los Cabal' and the rest of the letters are missing. And I don't see any cars. I think the town is gone."

"Turn here and maybe there will be more life when we get farther down this road," said Jane.

"Okey dokey," said Ashley, as she turned on the road toward the town. Everywhere they looked was brown and barren. The dirt kicked up off the road into a cloud as they drove along.

"It looks deserted to me," said Peaches, from the back seat. "I don't see the point of stopping here."

"Let's stop anyway. I just want to get out of the Jeep, and Edward probably needs to pee," said Ashley. "I'll stop in front of that old churchie-looking building."

"Churchie?" asked Jane.

"You know what I mean," said Ashley. "It looks like it used to be a church. A long, long time ago."

The old brown church building looked as though it was built from a combination of stone and adobe. It had a flat roof with rounded edges and thick walls. There was a tower section with windows and a crude looking cross on the top of it. The front door was missing and the windows were just rectangular openings with rounded tops. It looked as though no one had been here for a very long time.

Across the street was a rock building that looked like it was once a store. The sign was faded and the name couldn't be read. A wood-shingled roof was barely connected and was pitched at a crazy angle. There were several other buildings in varying stages of collapse, all in a row. They looked like they were built right up against each other.

"Most of these buildings look like they are from a long, long time ago," said Peaches, as Ashley drove slowly into the town. "They either fell down or burned down. I don't think there is anyone here anymore. They should call it Dust Town."

"I'm stopping here anyway and getting out. You can wait here if you want," said Ashley, as she stopped the Jeep and got out. "Let's go Edward!"

Edward jumped up from the back seat and

leaped out of the Jeep. He ran over to a scraggly-looking bush to pee, and ran back to Ashley wagging his tail. She took his bowl out from under the seat, poured water in it from her water bottle and set it down on the ground. Edward lapped up all of the water and sat down next to the Jeep.

Peaches and Jane also got out of the Jeep and stood up to stretch. "It does feel good to stretch," said Peaches. She pulled her camera out from the back seat. "I'm gonna take some pics. I've never been to a place like this before."

"Good idea," said Jane. "Let's go check out the cemetery next to the church."

"You know how I feel about cemeteries," said Ashley. "I'll stay here."

Peaches followed Jane toward the area to the left of the old church building. They stepped over a low stone wall to a grassy area with knee-high weeds and scattered headstones in varying sizes and shapes. Some were tilted, others were falling down, and some were laying flat on the ground. The writing, along with hearts and crosses, was etched into the stone slabs, darkened by time. Jane walked slowly past them, trying to read the names and words, but discovered they were in Spanish. Peaches had her camera out, snapping photos at every angle.

Jane walked back to the Jeep, while Peaches started wandering down the road taking various photos of the buildings and then came back to the join the rest of them. "I see a couple of cars down the street, and a pickup truck," she said.

"Then there must be some people around, but I don't think we want to go find out who they are," said Jane. "I know that's not likely to be the same white pickup truck I saw back home, but I'm avoiding all white pickup trucks."

"Oh, yeah. I remember," said Peaches. "It had a New Mexico license plate, didn't it? Maybe that's the one."

"That's another reason to avoid it," said Jane.

"It's kind of creepy here. I wonder how old this churchie-looking building is." She winked at Jane. Jane laughed.

"Probably hundreds of years," observed Ashley. "Hey, look! Now it looks like there are some lights on in there and someone is here. There's a glow coming out of the windows."

"I hear singing," said Jane.

"You hear singing all the time," said Ashley. "I'm going to peek in the window. Stay here, Edward." Edward sat back down beside the Jeep.

"We'll wait here, too," said Jane.

Ashley wandered up to a small side window and peered inside. It was still dark inside the building and she couldn't see very clearly except for what appeared to be lots of flickering candles causing the glow.

"Come here and look," she whispered loudly, waving Jane and Peaches over to the window. "There is something like a smoky cloud in there with twinkling lights."

Jane and Peaches ran over to the window to look. The three girls stood side-by-side peering through the open window, trying not to be seen from the inside. They watched and listened as the singing continued. Then they saw the twinkling lights transform into transparent images of people that spread out from the cloud and filled the room. A sudden burst of cold, damp air rushed out the window. The girls looked at each other with their eyes wide.

"That was weird! Let's get out of here," said Ashley, backing away from the window. The girls ran to the Jeep. Dust kicked up into a cloud behind them.

"Edward - in the Jeep! Your turn to drive, Jane," said Ashley, as she ran toward the passenger side. They all piled into the Jeep and headed back to the main road.

"I didn't get my ice cream," said Jane, as she turned on the main road and started to relax.

"Ha ha. I don't think there was any ice cream in that town. We'll find a real town soon. We just need to keep going," said Ashley. "I'll check the map."

"Um," said Peaches. "We did all see that, right?"

"See what?" said Jane and Ashley in unison, before they burst out laughing.

"Thought so," said Peaches. "Just checking."

Ten miles later, they found a small town with real stores and real people. Jane pulled in front of a store with a gas pump and Ashley filled the Jeep with gas. Jane found an ice cream shop and bought ice cream for everyone, including Edward. They were soon back on the road.

"Not much farther now," said Ashley.
"Great," said Jane.

CHAPTER FOURTEEN
SNAKE MOUNTAIN

WHEN THE GIRLS got back to the Emmons estate, Sarah was sitting in the porch swing, enjoying the afternoon.

"Hello, girls," said Sarah, as they approached the porch. "Hello, Edward."

Edward ran to Sarah wagging his tail and tried to lick her hands. She pulled them away and started patting him gently on the head. He sat down beside her to enjoy the attention, holding very still except for the thump of his tail as it wagged against the porch floor.

"Hi Sarah, thanks for the great breakfast," said Peaches. "You should open a bed and breakfast. You'd be really good at it."

Sarah laughed. "Maybe I should."

"We went to the Yellowglen Tribal Museum to show Jordan, the curator, these coins that I found in the cave," said Ashley. She held them out for Sarah to see. "Have you found any others like this?"

"No, I haven't. How interesting!" said Sarah.

"Here, they belong to you," said Ashley. "I found them in your cave."

"Thank you," said Sarah, as Ashley handed her the coins. "There have been rumors of a Spanish treasure hidden around here for as long as I can remember. But I've never seen anything to indicate that the stories were true."

Sarah studied the coins, holding them up to the light and looking at both sides. "The shapes are interesting," she said. "Almost like they were hand forged, and no two coins are alike."

"Yeah, they're nothing like the coins we have," said Ashley. "Did people make their own coins a long time ago?"

"I don't think so," said Sarah. "But I think that hundreds of years ago the process was much more primitive. I know that there were Spanish coins that were made in Mexico and South America back in the 1700s, and maybe earlier. I believe they were shipped back to Spain. Some of them didn't make it all the way to Spain. There are a large number of sunken treasure ships out in the ocean."

"Were they attacked by pirates?" asked Peaches.

"Not from what I've heard," said Sarah. "There were fleets of Spanish ships that sailed together at certain times of the year to avoid bad weather, like hurricanes. They also were heavily armed and guarded mainly so that they couldn't be robbed by ships from other countries."

"So there weren't really any pirates?" asked Peaches.

"I know there were pirates, and some pirates are well known, like Blackbeard, but I think most pirates usually would attack only single ships. The Spanish fleets stayed together for protection, but sometimes unexpected weather sunk them or they may have strayed into some rocks. I don't really know why they all sunk, but bad weather sunk more of the ships that were traveling back with goods from here than all of the pirates did. Hurricanes were the biggest problem."

"Were the ships full of coins?" asked Peaches.

"Not just coins. There was also gold and silver treasure, shaped into bars and religious and art pieces, and also trade goods and merchandise from both South America and Mexico," said Sarah. "There are dozens of sunken treasure ships in the waters around Florida, and the Bahamas, but they are in other places, too."

"It sounds like it was safer to stay here on land back then," said Peaches.

"Not really," said Sarah. "This was a tough place to live back in earlier centuries. There was a lot of ruthless conflict between the Spanish and the indigenous people who were here where we are now, and also in Mexico and South America. A lot of the conflict was because of the Spanish conquistadors searching for gold to send back to Spain. I know the Spanish brought the first horses here. The indigenous people who lived here had never seen horses before."

"So I bet the town called The Lost Horses must

have been built after the Spanish were here," said Peaches.

"What town is that?" asked Sarah, with a curious look on her face.

"Los Caballos Perdidos. I looked it up on my phone and it means The Lost Horses," said Peaches.

"That makes sense," said Sarah. "I don't think I've been there."

"You don't want to go there," said Ashley.

"Why not?" Sarah asked.

"We stopped there today and there's not much going on except an old church full of ghosts," Ashley replied.

"Ghosts?" asked Sarah.

"Yeah. They were singing in a church there. It was weird," said Ashley.

Sarah laughed. "If you lived here a while, you probably wouldn't think it was so unusual. This area dates back hundreds of years, and a lot of people have lived and died around here over all that time, often in some type of conflict, or in some cases, famine or disease. And when that happens, some spirits tend to hang around. Most of them mean no harm, so you don't need to be afraid of them. But they show up every once in a while, sometimes to help out, and other times, they just do their own thing," said Sarah.

Peaches and Jane looked at Ashley, but she didn't seem to want to say anything to Sarah about the American Indian man she saw in the cave. She gave them a look that indicated they should be quiet about it. Jane figured it wasn't her story to tell, so she kept mum about it.

"I could do some digging about the coins on my laptop," said Jane, changing the subject. "I brought it with me."

"Thank you, Jane," said Sarah. "Maybe you can find out more about when and where these were forged. "

"I'll try," said Jane.

"Did you find anything else?" asked Sarah.

"Just some skeletons and some old tools and a bucket," said Peaches.

"Oh," said Sarah. "Skeletons?"

"Yes," said Peaches. "I saw one of them and it was really creepy."

"I guess so," said Sarah with a chuckle. "Did they look like human skeletons, or were they animals?"

"I'd say they were human," said Peaches. "Really creepy humans."

"We'll probably need to report that to the sheriff," said Sarah. "They'll be able to figure out how long they might have been in there."

"I think it was probably a really long time," said Peaches.

"I would guess that, too, Peaches. So how do you know Jordan?" asked Sarah.

"We met him when we first arrived here. We went there to ask about the symbols on the sand paintings. He didn't know much about them, but sent us to a lady that did know something," said Jane.

"Oh good," said Sarah. "What did you find out?"

"Just that one of the symbols pointed to a place called Snake Mountain, and there were symbols showing a battle between Spanish men and some tribal warriors," Jane explained.

"Snake Mountain is right there," said Sarah, as she pointed up the hill. "I don't know much about what's up there, which is probably surprising for all the years I've lived here. I have ridden around that area on horseback, though. I love to ride, do any of you?"

"Ashley and I have ridden a few times with our families," said Jane.

"I never have," said Peaches. "But I'd love to try!"

"If you don't have other plans today, why don't you wander over to the stable and ask Dakota for a lesson and then you can go for a ride," Sarah suggested.

"That sounds fun!" said Peaches. "I'll go!"

Ashley shrugged her shoulders and looked at Jane. "Sound good?" she said.

"Sure," said Jane.

"Great," said Sarah. "The horses will love a chance to get out and about. Just head down that way toward the barn," she said as she pointed.

"Oh wait," said Ashley. "Edward can't ride. I'll stay here."

"Nonsense," said Sarah. "He can stay here with me."

"Are you sure?" said Ashley.

"Of course," said Sarah. "You go on now," she said, waving her hands. "He'll be fine."

"Okay, then," said Ashley. She gave Edward a squeeze. "You stay here with Sarah and be a good boy."

Edward whimpered and sat beside Sarah. His tail slowly thumped on the ground as it wagged.

The girls walked down to the horse barn to find Dakota. They walked into the main barn, past the twelve horse stalls and they didn't see anyone. After walking all the way through the barn, they found a large outdoor fenced arena behind it. There was small clubhouse next to the arena, with some outdoor tables and chairs under the overhang.

They wandered around outside until they found Dakota coming out of the clubhouse.

"Sarah sent us down here to ask for a riding lesson and said maybe we could take some horses out for a while. Do you have time?" said Jane.

"Of course," said Dakota. "Follow me into the barn." The girls followed him back into the barn, and just then a woman came out of one of the horse stalls.

"I put Chief back in his stall. I'm going back to the house," she said.

"Kaydee, I'd like you to meet Ms. Emmons' house guests. Jane, Peaches, and Ashley. This is my wife Kaydee," said Dakota.

"Nice to meet you girls," said Kaydee.

"Nice to meet you," said the girls.

"We came to ask Dakota for a riding lesson," said Peaches.

"He's a fine teacher," said Kaydee. "He'll show you what you need to know. He loves these horses and they love him."

"Good to know," said Jane.

Dakota selected three horses for the girls and spent an hour in the ring, instructing each of the girls on their horses.

"This is fun," said Peaches. "How did I live this long and never ride a horse before?"

"I don't know," said Jane.

"I think you girls are ready to go," said Dakota. "You can ride anywhere on the estate, but try not to stay out more than an hour. The horses will want to come back by then. There is a stream where they like to get a drink of water. Don't worry if they try to cross it. It's not very deep and they can handle it."

"I hope we don't get lost," said Ashley. "This estate is huge."

"They know the way back," said Dakota. "Just say 'home' and give them a little nudge with your heels, and they'll bring you back to the stable."

"That's handy!" said Peaches.

"They know the land, and they won't take you off the estate," said Dakota. "So, you should be fine by yourselves."

"Great. Thanks, Dakota. We'll see you in an hour," said Jane.

They started off with a slow trot. It wasn't long before the girls started to feel comfortable in the saddle.

"This is so much fun!" said Peaches.

"Yeah, I love it," said Ashley.

"Let's go up to Snake Mountain, while we have

a way to get there," said Jane. "I want to see what's up there."

"I'm curious, too," said Ashley. "Let's do it!"

"I hope there aren't any snakes," said Peaches.

"They won't be able to reach you up on a horse," said Jane.

"Oh, good point," said Peaches.

The girls rode for a while in silence, taking in the beauty of the landscape around them. They had never seen such a picturesque place in person. Surrounded by beautiful blue sky with wispy white clouds as far as they could see across the flat desert land, it didn't seem real. The mountain range loomed large in the background against the flat surface.

"The clouds look like feathers," noted Peaches.

"Hey, yeah, they kinda do," agreed Jane.

The first part of the ride was fairly easy. There was mostly flat ground with small shrubs and not too many rocks, and there was a trail they could follow. There weren't enough clouds to block the warmth of the sun, which made it pretty warm out there. They were prepared with water bottles that Dakota provided. He said they would need plenty of water, and he was right. They stopped a few times to take a drink before they reached the stream for the horses.

The farther they rode, the hillier it became, and they encountered more trees as they traveled farther from the house. Ponderosa pines, box elders, fir, and many other trees provided more shade as they cantered toward the mountain, which made the ride more pleasant.

The horses slowed down to a trot as they approached more trees.

"I think I saw a coyote," said Ashley.

"Where?" said Jane.

"He just ran past that tree ahead of us," said Ashley.

"I see the stream ahead," said Peaches, pointing to it. "It's beautiful."

"We should go let the horses get a drink," said Jane. They all trotted toward the stream. After the horses drank some water, the girls crossed the stream. They followed alongside the stream for a while until they saw a narrow, steep-walled canyon cut into the side of the mountain.

"How cool is this?" said Ashley. "Do you think this was here naturally or did someone dig out a shelter in the side of the mountain?"

"I have no idea," said Jane. "That's a good question for Dr. Parker. But I bet some people lived in here at one time. It would be good protection from the weather."

Peaches pulled out her camera and took some photos of it. She spotted a large amount of boulders in one spot on the right side of the cavern and zoomed in for a close-up. Looking into her viewfinder, she could make out '1652' carved into a ledge above the rocks.

"Look at this," she said. "The numbers '1652' are carved into the ledge above that bunch of boulders over there." Jane and Ashley looked where she was pointing.

"Let's go check it out," said Ashley. She

started riding toward it, and her horse stopped abruptly. "What's the matter?" she said, digging her heels into the horse's side. "Go." The horse wouldn't budge.

Jane and Peaches had stopped behind her, when Ashley's horse had stopped. Ashley looked down and saw a large area scattered with snakes. Some of the closest ones were rattling their tails. "Uh oh," said Ashley.

"What do you see?" said Jane.

"Lots and lots of snakes," said Ashley. "I think they're rattlers."

"We're done with this," said Peaches. "I'm not fighting off snakes to see what's over there. I have a pic of it. I'll look at it later." She turned her horse around and headed back toward the stream. Ashley and Jane followed her.

They traveled a bit farther down the stream past the canyon, and soon they were ascending almost straight up the mountain, as the elevation had changed drastically.

At this point, Jane started to hear something rhythmic. "Wait, slow down a minute," she said. They all came to a stop. "Do you hear that?"

"Hear what?" said Peaches. "More rattlesnakes?"

"No. The drum beat. I hear drumming and chanting," said Jane. "Listen."

"I don't hear anything," said Ashley. "You've said that before. Maybe something's wrong with your hearing."

"There's nothing wrong with my hearing. I hear native drumming and singing," said Jane. She turned her horse in the direction of the drumming. Then it sounded like it was behind her, so she turned again and took a few steps.

"Well, we don't hear it," said Peaches.

"No one else ever hears it," said Ashley.

"Well, I do. But when I step in the direction of the sound, it changes and then sounds like it's coming from a different direction."

"Okay," said Ashley. "Let's just keep going."

"This is getting kinda steep," said Peaches. "I hope the horses can handle it."

"Just go slow," said Ashley.

"Maybe we should turn back," said Jane. "It's almost straight up at this point."

Ashley spotted an open area among the trees, with some rocks piled up on a slope. "Wait, I want to see something. Those rocks are a darker color than the surrounding area," she said. She slid down off her horse and handed the reins to Jane.

Ashley walked over towards the slope to investigate. She saw a piece of metal stuck in the rocks and picked it up. "This looks like a spur," she said. She walked back to the horses and handed it to Peaches. "Here hold this," she said. Peaches tucked the spur in her pocket.

Ashley went back to the pile of rocks and started moving them to a new pile. "This slope looks like it could be another cave or maybe someone is buried here. I wanna see what it is."

"Buried?" said Jane. "I sure hope not."

"Watch out for the snakes," Peaches warned.

Ashley laughed, and kept on moving the rocks. "Like that one?" she said, pointing. A large king snake eased out from one of the rocks.

"Ewww," said Peaches.

Ashley grabbed it with both hands, keeping the head away from her. She stood up and walked over to a nearby tree and deposited the snake away from where she was working. She walked back over to the pile of rocks.

"That's not your first snake, is it?" asked Jane.

"No, it's not," said Ashley. "It's just a king snake. Nothing to worry about."

"Unless it scares me to death," said Peaches.

"I guess that's possible," said Ashley with a chuckle.

"I didn't think you were afraid of anything," said Jane.

"Only snakes," said Peaches. "Not people."

Ashley got down on her knees and peered into an opening that the rocks had been covering. All of a sudden, the ground gave way under her and she tumbled about thirty feet underground into a slanted shaft.

Jane gasped. "Wha?"

"O M G, Jane, O M G," said Peaches, with her hand covering her mouth.

Jane immediately slid down from her horse and handed the reins to Peaches. "Ash, Ash, are you okay?" she called, as she ran towards the slope. She stayed back a few feet to be sure she didn't also fall into the hole.

"I'm okay," called Ashley. "It wasn't straight down. It was kinda like a cool slide."

"That's a relief. We need to get you out of there," said Jane.

"Wait, maybe I can climb back up," said Ashley.

She tried multiple times to climb back up the shaft, but she kept sliding back down. "Are there any vines or anything you can use to pull me up?"

Jane looked around. "No, I don't see anything like that."

"I guess I can't get back up on my own then."

"Peaches can go back to the house and get Dakota and Andy, and I'll stay here with you," said Jane.

"Okay?" said Jane, as she turned her head towards Peaches.

"Sure, I'll go," said Peaches. "Take these horses."

Jane walked over and took the reins of the two horses from Peaches. She looked around for the closest small tree and tied the reins to the tree.

"We'll be right here," Jane said to Peaches. "Look around so you can remember where we are."

Peaches looked around for a minute. "Got it," she said. "Home!" she said to the horse, and nudged her horse gently with her heels. The horse took off trotting toward the stable.

Jane sat down on the ground near the opening

to wait. "Are you okay?" she called.

"I'm good," said Ashley. "I have my cell phone, so I'm going to use the flashlight to look around."

"Okay, I'll be waiting here," said Jane. "Be careful."

"Got it, I will," said Ashley.

CHAPTER FIFTEEN

HOLES AND PASSAGEWAYS

"JANE?" CALLED ASHLEY.

"Yeah, I'm still here," said Jane.

"It looks like there is a large room down here with stone walls built in layers with mortar. There are also several smaller rooms. There are some carvings on one of the cave walls and there is a passageway leading somewhere."

"Really? Wow."

"Yeah. I'm going to poke around the passageway a little bit. It looks sturdy enough."

"Okay, I guess. Be careful," said Jane.

Jane sat and waited for a long time. Eventually Peaches showed up with Dakota and Andy. Dakota had a long rope tied to his saddle.

Jane was relieved to see them. "I'm so glad to see you. Ashley went exploring and I haven't heard from her in a while."

She walked back over to the opening. "Ash?

Ashley?" she called.

No answer.

Peaches tried. "Ashley?" she yelled.

No answer.

Just then Jane's cell phone rang. "Wha?" said Jane. "It looks like she's calling me."

She clicked the button to answer her phone. "Ashley?" she said.

"It's me!" said Ashley.

"Where are you?" said Jane.

"I'm outside!" she said. "Near the place where we escaped from the cave the other day. Can you come here?"

"Sure, I guess," said Jane.

"See you in a few," said Ashley and she hung up.

Jane turned to the others. "She said she is out of the cave and she's near the exit from the other cave," said Jane.

Everyone looked confused.

"Okay then," said Andy. "Let's go there. Follow me."

Dakota untied the horses from the tree, and handed one set to Jane. He waited to make sure she could get back on her horse, and held onto the other ones from Ashley's horse as he mounted his horse.

"Let's go," he said.

They all followed Andy to the other cave. When they arrived, Ashley was sitting on a large boulder outside the cave with a big smile on her face.

"You're not gonna believe it! You're just not gonna believe it!" said Ashley. She jumped up from the boulder.

"Believe what?" said Andy.

"It's all one cave!" said Ashley. "I followed the passageway and it came out right here."

"How far was it?" asked Jane.

"Far," said Ashley. "Really far and really dark and cold. And wet, too. There are small ponds in there and rocks, and I think I saw some bats."

"That's strange but not surprising. Who knows what's on this land? Many generations of people have lived here," Andy said. "I'm glad you're okay."

"Thanks for coming to help," said Ashley. "I'm fine and don't need rescuing today."

"What's that?" asked Peaches, pointing to the glass bottle in Ashley's hand.

"Just a cool bottle I found," said Ashley.

"Here's your horse," said Dakota, handing the reins to Ashley. "Let's head back to the stable."

"Thanks," said Ashley. "Here hold this for a minute," she said, as she handed the bottle to Peaches. Ashley mounted her horse and Peaches handed the bottle back to Ashley. They all followed Dakota back to the stable. The girls walked their horses back into the stable and helped put them away.

"Thanks for a great adventure today, and the riding lesson, too," said Jane.

"Yes, thanks Dakota," said Peaches.

"We need to get back to the house," said Ashley. "I don't want Edward to think I abandoned him."

"Let's go," said Peaches.

On the way back to the house, Ashley couldn't contain herself. "I have to tell you what I found. You're just not gonna believe it."

"What? The glass bottle?" said Jane.

"More ghosts?" said Peaches.

"Treasure... gold treasure," she said. "Lots of it. Stacks of gold and silver bars, about a thousand of them, and some bags of coins." She pulled out gold and silver coins from her pocket just like the others she had found.

"Did you bring one of the gold bars?" asked Peaches.

"No, they were too heavy. I tried to pick one up, but I didn't know how I was going to get out of there, so I left it there," replied Ashley. "It must have weighed 40 or 50 pounds."

"One gold bar weighed 50 pounds?" asked Peaches.

"Yes, just one bar was too heavy to carry through the cave," said Ashley. "It wasn't like I could put it in my pocket. But I did take a picture with my phone."

"Why didn't you say something before?" said Jane.

"I didn't know who we could trust," said Ashley. "Someone's been after us, and we don't know who."

"True," said Jane.

"And this glass bottle has something in it. It's a

rolled-up sheepskin with writing on it. It looked like it might be Spanish," said Ashley. "I put it back in the bottle."

"What do we do now?" said Peaches. "Do we tell Sarah, or do we tell my dad first?"

"That's a good question," said Jane. "Hmmm." She thought about it as they walked along.

"I think we need to trust her and tell her," said Jane. "After all, it's on her property. She's taken good care of us. I don't think she would have anything to do with whoever broke into the Archaeology lab and hurt Carl, stole the photos back home, and whoever pushed me in front of a car and/or trashed our hotel room. That had to be someone else."

"That makes sense. Also, Edward likes her. That's a good sign. He's a good judge of character," said Ashley.

"Yeah, I agree," said Peaches.

When they approached the house, Edward and Sarah were sitting on the porch.

"Have you been here the whole time we were gone?" asked Jane.

"Goodness, no," said Sarah. "We went inside for a bit, but just came out because we thought it was about time for you to be back. How was your ride?"

"It was fun!" said Peaches. "This land is beautiful. It's like nowhere I've ever been before. Like a postcard."

"It never ceases to amaze me with its beauty," said Sarah. "I can't imagine living anywhere else. The beautiful sunrises and sunsets are the best part."

"I might even get up early to see the sunrise," said Peaches. "I hadn't thought of what it would like from here. I bet it's amazing."

"You won't be disappointed," said Sarah, nodding her head. "You could get some photos with your camera."

"Yeah, good idea," agreed Peaches.

"Sarah, we have something to tell you," said Jane.

"Oh? What is it?" said Sarah.

"While we were out riding, Ashley fell in a hole up on the mountain," said Jane.

"Oh dear," said Sarah. "How did that happen?"

"I saw some rocks piled up and was curious. I was moving them to see what was behind them and the earth gave out under me. I slid down into a large room underground," said Ashley.

"Are you okay?" said Sarah.

"Yes, I'm fine. It was slanted like a big slide. I wasn't hurt."

"That's good," said Sarah.

"While I was down there, I poked around and found a large room with walls built out of stones. Someone put a lot of effort into building that room."

"It sounds like it," said Sarah.

"Anyhoo… in the room were stacks of gold bars and some bags of gold coins. The coins are like the ones I gave you that I found in the cave."

She pulled the coins out of her pocket. "Here," she said. "These are yours, too."

Sarah took the coins and looked closely at

them.

"You found gold bars, too?" she said.

"Yes, lots of 'em. I even took a pic with my phone, because I didn't know if anyone would believe it." Ashley pulled out her cell phone and showed Sarah the photo.

"Oh my," she gasped, covering her hand over her mouth.

"And this bottle. It has something in it – a sheepskin or something with writing on it," said Ashley, as she handed the bottle to Sarah.

"You should know, Sarah, that someone has been following us, so we are concerned about who can be trusted with this information," said Jane.

"Someone was following you?" she asked. "Who?"

"I didn't mean anyone was following me in the cave," said Ashley.

"Someone has been lurking around ever since we were in Ohio. I don't know who it is," said Jane. "But they broke into Dr. Parker's lab and stole the sand paintings that he found here in your cave. Then he printed some photos that he had taken of them, and someone stole the photos off the table in a restaurant where we were discussing it. Then someone was following us back to campus. Then, on my way to the library, someone pushed me out in front of a car."

"And you have no idea who it was?" asked Sarah.

"Peaches saw a man with jeans and a tee shirt with brown hair that grabbed the photos, and it looked like it might have been him that followed us back to the campus, but that's all we know. Then when we came here to the Yellowglen Tribal Museum to ask Jordan about the sand paintings, someone trashed our hotel room," said Jane.

"That's when my dad called you and asked if we could stay here," said Peaches.

"I see," said Sarah.

"So, we just want to be careful with this information about what Ash found in the cave," said Jane.

"I get it," said Sarah. "I don't know much about digging treasure out of a cave, so I am going to contact Dr. Parker and get him involved. We need an archaeologist who knows what he's doing."

"That's a great idea," said Jane.

"We've had people hanging around over the years looking for the Spanish treasure. I just thought it was an old story. I didn't think it was real. Maybe this could be it," said Sarah.

"Tell her who you saw in the cave yesterday," said Peaches.

"Who do you mean?" asked Ashley.

"The guy. You know. The one that showed you how to get out," said Peaches.

"I wasn't planning on telling anyone else about that," said Ashley, looking embarrassed.

"Go ahead and tell her," urged Jane. "I'd like to hear what Sarah thinks about it."

"Well, okay," said Ashley reluctantly. "I was trying to find a way out of the cave, when I saw a man in the cave that looked like an American Indian. He motioned to me to follow him, so I did. I could see him, even though it was dark. He had a glow around him. Edward and I followed him for a bit and then he showed us the spot where some sunlight was peeking into the cave. He stood beside it and pointed to it. That's how we found a way out. As soon as I saw it, the man disappeared."

Sarah grinned and started laughing out loud and nodding.

"See, why did you make me tell her?" Ashley asked, looking even more embarrassed.

"I'm sorry," said Sarah. "I was laughing because I know exactly who you saw. We used to call him Chief Goodfeather. My brother and I saw him all the time when I was a child, when we were playing outside on this land."

"You've seen him, too?" said Peaches.

"Yes, many times," said Sarah. "I used to see him just standing around watching when my brother and I were playing in the yard. Once we wandered too far from the house and got lost. There he was, motioning for us to follow him and he led us back home safe and sound. I haven't seen him in many years, though."

"Did you see him in the cave today, too?" asked Peaches.

"No, he wasn't there today," said Ashley.

"I'm glad he's still around, though," said Jane. "He probably saved our lives when we were trapped in that cave."

"I'm glad, too," said Sarah, remembering him fondly. "He's never given me any reason to be afraid of him. He just shows up sometimes, so I think he may always be around."

"I'll go give Dr. Parker a call. How much longer are you girls on Fall Break from school?"

"Just a few more days," said Jane. "Classes start again on Monday. I was thinking we need to start heading back tomorrow, but now that Ashley found this treasure, I'd like to wait to find out what Dr. Parker says."

"Agreed," said Peaches, nodding her head. "I'm not going anywhere until we find out what happens next."

"When do you have to be back, Ashley?" asked Jane.

"I don't start my new job for a few weeks," said Ashley.

"What is your new job?" asked Sarah.

"I'm going to be a basketball coach at West Midland High School," said Ashley with a smile.

"That's a perfect job for you," said Jane.

"I know, right?" said Ashley. "It's going to be fun to coach a girls' basketball team and they're going to pay me for it."

"I guess we're here a few more days," said Jane. She shrugged her shoulders. "I hope that's okay."

"That's great," said Sarah. "I'm enjoying having you girls visit."

"Thanks," said Jane.

CHAPTER SIXTEEN

DR. PARKER ARRIVES

IT WAS LATE AFTERNOON the next day when Dr. Parker, along with Chris and Kendra, the two graduate students, arrived at the Emmons estate, ready for action.

Dr. Parker was dressed in field clothes appropriate for the desert climate. Even though it's fairly warm in New Mexico in the fall, he wore light colored clothing with long sleeves and long pants that were lightweight and dried quickly, to protect him from the sun. He also had sturdy boots and a bucket hat.

Chris was wearing his typical daily garb - denim overalls, tee shirt and boots, with his long brown hair pulled back in a bright orange bandana. He unloaded a backpack with a folded-up hat and a water bottle in the side pockets and a five-gallon water jug, along with three duffel bags and a tool bucket from Dr. Parker's pickup truck.

Kendra also wore a bucket hat, and a lightweight

long sleeve shirt and long pants and bright yellow utility vest. She was carrying a backpack and camera case.

"Thanks for coming so quickly," said Sarah. "It's nice to see you all again. However, it makes me nervous that there has been someone following the girls around, knowing there may be a Spanish treasure buried here. I don't want anyone else getting hurt."

"I agree," said Dr. Parker. "I'd like to get this handled as safely and efficiently as we can."

"How is your teaching assistant doing?" asked Sarah.

"He's getting better," said Dr. Parker. "He was hurt pretty badly. He just needs some time to heal."

"I'm glad to hear he is okay. He's a nice young man," said Sarah.

"It's nice that we already have the tents and site already set up," said Dr. Parker. "That will make things a little easier."

"You should be aware that someone pulled back some of the tarps and dug around a bit at the excavation site. I don't know who it was but it happened the day after the girls arrived. We haven't tried to fix it, so you'll be able to see what they did."

"That's worrisome," said Dr. Parker. "I've contacted the sheriff to make sure we have some protection while we are doing our work. Another truck will be arriving first thing tomorrow and we'll get started in the morning."

"Since you only have two students with you, I have room for the three of you at my house this time.

That is, if you and Chris can bunk together, I have another room for Kendra," said Sarah.

"Thanks so much," said Dr. Parker. "We can do that. It'll be better if we all stay close together, now that there is a possible treasure involved."

"I agree," said Sarah. "You can go ahead and take your things into the house," she said to Chris and Kendra, "and please make yourselves at home. There is lemonade in the kitchen."

"Thank you, ma'am" said Kendra. Chris nodded and started carrying the rest of their gear into the house.

As they all entered the front door, Sarah said, "Oh, and I do have something to show you. Come with me, Jerome."

Dr. Parker followed her into the room with the fireplace. Sarah reached into one of the display cases and pulled out the glass bottle.

"Ashley found this in the cave with the gold," she said as she handed him the bottle.

"Interesting!" He pulled the rolled-up sheepskin partway out of the bottle. "This looks like sheepskin. That could help us identify an origin and a time frame. Mind if I take this bottle with me to study it?"

"Of course, that's fine," said Sarah.

"And these gold coins, too," said Sarah. She grabbed the coins from the shelf where she had left them and held them out for him to see. "Jane volunteered to do some research on the coins on her laptop. I'm not sure if she has found out anything yet."

"Great!" said Dr. Parker. "She's really started showing a keen interest in Archaeology. I'll have to ask her what she found. If you'll spread these coins out under the light, I'll just take some pictures of them and leave the coins here with you."

Sarah spread the coins out on the shelf and Dr. Parker took several photos. He also took the sheepskin out of the bottle and spread it out and took a photo of it. He also took photos of the bottle and the writing on the bottle. Then he rolled the sheepskin back up and put it back in the bottle.

"The writing on it is Spanish. On second thought, I'll just leave this bottle with you, as well, and use the pictures to research it later. I think that'll be safer than me carrying it around. Now, who can show me the location where all this gold was found?" said Dr. Parker.

"Probably Ashley is the best one to show you. She found it after accidentally falling into a back entrance to the cave. It's the same cave that is next to the excavation site, but it turned out to be a very large cave. If you head down that way," she said, as she pointed to the stable, "Dakota can mount you up on a horse, and I'll send Ashley down there, too. She can lead you to the opening of the cave and describe what is down there."

"A horse?" said Dr. Parker.

"Yes, have you ridden a horse before?" asked Sarah. "It's the best way to get to the other end of the cave. It's up on Snake Mountain. It's much too far to walk."

"Yes, I have ridden a horse before, but it's been a while," said Dr. Parker.

"Dakota can help you," said Sarah. "Tell him I'd like for him to accompany you, as well."

"Okay," said Dr. Parker. "Thank you, Sarah. You've been so welcoming and helpful to the girls, and to the students. I really appreciate everything."

"I'm happy to have your help with this, Jerome," said Sarah. "I wouldn't know who else to call."

Dr. Parker headed down to the stable, and Sarah sent Ashley on her way there, too. Sarah, Peaches, Jane and Edward waited for them back at the house. Chris and Kendra went to check on the excavation site and began putting things back where they belong.

"Let's go check out the dig site, while we wait," said Jane. "Chris and Kendra already went out there. I want to see what they're doing."

"Okay, I guess," said Peaches. "I already looked under one of the tarps and it was just some dirt."

"C'mon, Edward," said Jane. They were keeping an eye on him while Ashley was off with Dr. Parker. He jumped up and wagged his tail, ready to go.

Jane and Peaches walked out to the site with Edward. They found Chris and Kendra neatly staking the tarps back the way they were originally. The small trailer was unlocked and it looked as though someone had dug through the drawers of the file cabinet.

"How's it look?" asked Jane.

"Not too bad," Kendra answered. "So far it

looks as though someone was doing some digging, and didn't care about the mess they made. Our work is very precise and careful, and it makes me mad that someone was so rude and careless."

"If they want to know what we found, they should just ask us," Chris added. "We'd be happy to show anyone that is interested. It's not a secret."

"I guess they didn't want you to know they wanted to know, whoever they are," said Peaches. "Hey, I almost forgot. We found a spur up on the mountain. Do you want to see it?"

"Sure," said Chris. "We'd love to take a look at it."

"Don't let me forget when we're back at the house to show it to you. I forgot to give it to Sarah after Ashley fell in the cave and all that commotion," said Peaches.

It was about an hour later when Ashley and Dr. Parker arrived back at the house to find everyone sitting on the front porch, enjoying the evening air and watching the sun begin to set. The purple and amber haze below the clouds flooded the open landscape.

"This sunset is so beautiful," said Peaches. "I just can't get enough of it. It's like a live postcard every evening."

"I never get tired of it," said Sarah, nodding in agreement.

Edward jumped up to greet Ashley, wagging his tail wildly. She guided him over to the side of the porch and sat down beside him and gave him a big hug around his neck.

"What do you think?" asked Sarah, as Dr. Parker stepped up onto the porch. "Can you manage it all?"

"I have to say I'm dumbfounded," said Dr. Parker. "What an incredible find. If Ashley hadn't been curious about that pile of rocks, it might have never been found," said Dr. Parker.

"I've lived here all my life and never had any idea it was there," said Sarah. "Of course, I've heard rumors of Spanish treasure, but didn't know where it was or if it was true."

"People have found Spanish treasure in multiple places and various mines and I've heard many, many stories over the years. I did hear one story about some men who brought a large stash of gold from South America back in the 1930s, and buried it somewhere in the southwestern U.S. to wait for its value to increase. But then the next year they passed a law banning the individual ownership of gold bullion by U.S. citizens, so they were never able to sell it."

"They must have been very disappointed," said Sarah.

"No doubt," said Dr. Parker with a knowing smile. "From 1933 to 1974 it was illegal to own gold bullion without a special license. But then a more recent law passed allowing it again, so it's just as well that it stayed hidden all this time if this is their stash. I imagine the men that buried it died long ago, if the story is true."

"Lucky me!" said Sarah. "Maybe this is the gold they buried."

"Indeed," said Dr. Parker with a smile of satisfaction. "Anything is possible."

Peaches suddenly jumped up. "I almost forgot!" She ran into the house and came right back out. "I wanted to show you the spur we found up on the mountain." She handed it to Chris.

Kendra leaned over to look at it as Chris turned it every which way in his hand. He tried to brush some of the dirt off to see what it was made from. "The shank is very ornate," he said.

"It might be silver," said Kendra.

"It might," agreed Chris. "I've seen this shape of this shank before. And look at the work they did on this band. I'd guess it's from the Spanish conquistadors. The Spanish brought horses here. This could be pretty old."

"That's a great find," said Dr. Parker. "Where was it?"

"It was up on Snake Mountain. Ashley found it when she was moving rocks, along with a big ol' snake," said Peaches.

Ashley laughed. "It was just a king snake. I guess it knew where it was supposed to live. Snake Mountain, right?"

Sarah and Dr. Parker laughed. "Makes sense," said Sarah. "I told the girls I've rarely gone up to the mountain, and only on horseback, so I have no idea what's there."

"I don't think we'll have time to look around up there on this trip," said Dr. Parker. "But seems like we should at some point."

"When you do, watch out for the rattlesnake cavern," said Peaches.

"Rattlesnake cavern?" said Dr. Parker.

"Yeah. When we were out riding, we found a cavern cut into the mountain that looks like maybe people lived there. But now it's full of rattlesnakes," said Peaches.

"Oh my. I'm glad no one was hurt," said Sarah.

"We stayed on the horses and turned around when we saw them. But I took some pics. Inside the cavern, there's a big pile of boulders and it has '1652' carved into a ledge at the top of them," said Peaches.

"Wait a minute," said Jane. "I just remembered something. I'll be right back." Jane ran into the house to her room and came back with the folded piece of paper that she had found when they were trapped in the cave.

"I found this when we were trapped in the cave the other day," said Jane. "It looks like a old map drawing with maybe some roads or trails marked on it. But then it shows an opening with 1652 written above it, just like Peaches said she saw in the cavern."

"Let me see," said Dr. Parker. Jane handed him the paper.

"This is really interesting," said Dr. Parker. "Later we can compare it with your photo, Peaches. However, we won't be able to explore it any further on this trip. Sarah, do you want to hold onto this for now?"

"Of course." Sarah tucked it into her skirt pocket.

"Your land seems to be full of mysteries," said Dr. Parker.

"It certainly does," said Sarah. "Andy will be back shortly," said Sarah. "He can help with whatever you need tomorrow."

"That will be great," said Dr. Parker. "I could use his help managing things."

Two sheriff's deputies showed up at the door.

"Thank you for coming, guys," said Dr. Parker.

"Hi, I am Deputy Dave Robbins, and this is my partner, Luis Vasquez."

Dr. Parker explained about the vandalism at the excavation site, and the plan for the next day. "Another truck will be here in the morning with some men and equipment to help us haul everything out of the cave. We'll probably need to make a few trips to the bank, and we'll need one of you to accompany the truck and one to stay here. I've arranged with the local bank to store everything in the vault until I can arrange to have it picked up," said Dr. Parker.

"Got it," said Deputy Dave. "We've got you covered."

"Let me know whatever you need from me," said Andy, who had just come out the front door to join them.

"Great," said Dr. Parker. "We need to decide the best way to extract the bars from the cave. Will it be better to pull it up the shaft and haul it down from the mountain, or load it up from inside the cave and bring it out of the other opening? Can you come take a look with me and help me size up the situation?"

"Of course," said Andy. "Let's take my Jeep and we'll drive to both locations and survey the situation. We'll see what the landscape looks like in between the openings."

Dr. Parker laughed. "Great! I wasn't looking forward to spending the day on a horse."

"Oh, yeah," chuckled Andy. "That won't be necessary."

"If you don't need anything else from us tonight, we will be here first thing tomorrow," said Deputy Dave.

"Great," said Dr. Parker. "Thanks! See you tomorrow."

CHAPTER SEVENTEEN
KAYDEE'S WARNING

THE NEXT MORNING a large, gray and green paneled truck arrived with two men. On the side it said, "R&B Excavation Service LLC." Dr. Parker hired them to help get the gold out of the cave and take it to the bank. He was up early to greet them and helped them haul some equipment out of the truck.

The two deputies arrived right behind the truck. "Thanks for coming, guys," said Dr. Parker. He introduced the deputies to Bubba and Rick, the men in the truck. "This is the truck we'll be using to take the gold to the bank vault," he explained.

Jane was in the kitchen eating breakfast before anyone else was up. Sarah, as usual, had a great breakfast spread waiting for all of them. She had already gone outside to talk to Dr. Parker and the men when Jane had awakened.

Chris and Kendra both came out of their rooms and sat down with Jane at the table.

"This is great!" said Kendra. "I won't want to leave here this time."

"I know, right?" said Jane. "Sarah is the best hostess I can imagine."

"Last time we slept in tents and had to cook for ourselves," said Kendra. "There aren't any hotels nearby, so that was the only real option for 12 of us. It was okay, but this is awesome." She picked up an empty coffee cup and Jane handed her the pot of coffee.

"Thanks," said Kendra, taking the pot. She poured herself a cup of coffee, and then held it out to Chris. Chris nodded and took the pot from her and poured his coffee and handed it back to Jane. He dumped a few spoonfuls of sugar into his cup and then added some milk and started stirring it.

"Is that like hot coffee ice cream?" asked Kendra, with a chuckle.

Chris smiled. "Kinda, I guess. That's how I like it."

Kendra laughed.

"You and Peaches have a lot in common," said Jane. "She drinks a little coffee with her cream and sugar, too."

Chris laughed. "It's good like this! You should try it."

Jane laughed, too. "What are you two doing today?" she asked. "Is there anything I can do to help you?"

"We're not sure exactly," said Chris. "Dr. Parker wants us to come up to the mountain to see what we can do to help. We've already finished putting the excavation site back together."

"Oh, okay. I guess I'll ask him then," said Jane. "Was there anything missing from the dig site or did someone just look through it?" asked Jane.

"There wasn't really anything there anymore," said Chris. "It looked like someone was just snooping around."

Edward's toenails clicked on the tile floor, as he trotted out to the kitchen with Ashley following. "Edward heard people talking and wanted to know what was going on," said Ashley, yawning and rubbing her eyes.

Edward wagged his tail and sniffed Chris and Kendra. "Looks like he likes the two of you," Ashley confirmed.

"Well, that's good," said Kendra. "Hi boy," she said. Edward sat down beside her and put his head in her lap. Kendra chuckled.

Ashley poured herself a glass of orange juice and sat down with them at the table. She started munching on a doughnut, still trying to wake up. "So, what are we doing today?" she asked.

"I'm not sure," said Jane. "I'll ask Dr. Parker if we can help."

Just then, the hinges on the wood-framed front door squeaked as it opened. Sarah walked in with Kaydee and Dakota. Kaydee seemed upset.

"What do you think is going to happen?" Sarah asked.

"Bad things. Evil things. You must not dig on

sacred land," said Kaydee.

"Dr. Parker isn't doing any digging this time," explained Sarah. "They are just going to bring some items out of the cave up on the mountain. I don't understand what you're telling me."

"The mountain is sacred land," said Kaydee. "There was a battle there and warriors are buried there. They must not be disturbed or evil things will happen."

Sarah turned to Jane. "Jane, will you go out and ask Dr. Parker to come in here, please?"

"Sure," said Jane. She got up and went outside to get Dr. Parker. When she went outside, she saw that the two men in the paneled truck had pulled out a UTV (Utility Terrain Vehicle) with a wagon attached and were driving away in it towards the mountain.

"Dr. Parker, Sarah would like to see you inside," said Jane.

"Okay, I'll be right there."

Jane went back in the house and let Sarah know he was coming in. Kaydee looked upset and frustrated, and Dakota was standing quietly beside her.

The front door squeaked again. "You wanted to see me?" asked Dr. Parker as he entered the front door.

"Yes, thank you," said Sarah. "Kaydee, please explain again what you are telling me to Dr. Parker."

"The mountain is sacred land," said Kaydee. "There was a battle there and warriors are buried there. They must not be disturbed or evil things will happen."

"A battle?" asked Dr. Parker.

"Yes, we have found many signs. Signs of

Spanish warriors and our ancestors that have died in battle on this mountain."

"You don't mean down here near the house by the dig site, but up the hill on Snake Mountain?" asked Dr. Parker.

"Yes, yes, on the mountain. You must not dig there. Many bones are buried there and some that are no longer buried," pleaded Kaydee. "They must not be disturbed."

"What kinds of things have you found?" asked Dr. Parker.

"We have found a few bones when we were out riding on the mountain. They look like they could be human bones," said Dakota. "We've also found pieces of Spanish armor, spurs, a metal knife, part of a tomahawk, and a few coins. Also, many arrowheads. The way things were scattered around, it seems that there was a battle. If you have found something in the cave, is it more coins?"

Dr. Parker raised his eyebrows. "You found coins?" asked Dr. Parker.

"Yes, a few Spanish coins," said Dakota. "That convinced us that this was a battle with Spanish men and that they might have hidden a treasure on the mountain. We have heard many stories about that."

"What?" asked Sarah. "I didn't know about this."

"Kaydee found some coins last Spring up on the mountain when she was horseback riding. She took them to town to find out what they were, and realized that the Spanish treasure we heard so much about must have been somewhere on this land. Like I said, over the years we have been riding horses on this land, we've found indications that the Spaniards were here – spurs and such, and also human bones up on the mountain. It was clear that there had been a battle here."

Dr. Parker turned to Dakota. "I assure you both that we will not disturb any bones, and I will contact the authorities about any human bones we encounter, so they can be reburied. I do not wish to disturb sacred ground, but I think we can extract any treasure we find without doing so," he said. "We will not be performing any digging on the mountain."

"I warned you," said Kaydee. "That's all I can do." She turned and walked out of the house and back to the stable cottage.

"I hope nothing happens," said Dakota. "But I don't know. I must go now." He turned and left.

"We'll do our best," Dr. Parker assured Sarah. "I can call someone to help with this. Trust me."

"I know you will," said Sarah. "Let's get this done."

Dr. Parker pulled out his cell phone and stepped outside to make a call. He came back into the kitchen.

"I'll need everyone to meet me at the cave entrance where Ashley fell in about 30 minutes," said Dr. Parker. "Sarah, you don't need to come, since you won't be doing any of the physical work on this."

"Okay," said Sarah. Everyone else got up from the table and went to get dressed for the day. Jane roused Peaches and got her moving as well. Sarah let

Andy know. Ashley and Andy drove the crew in their Jeeps to the mountain, where they spotted the excavation guys setting up their equipment.

A few minutes later, a black two-door Jeep arrived with someone Jane didn't recognize. The man driving the Jeep stepped out and stood beside it looking around. He looked like an American Indian with dark reddish-brown skin and long straight black hair pulled back into a braid. He was neatly dressed in a short-sleeved collared shirt with an exquisite looking Native American bolo tie. It had a beautiful oblong center piece that looked as though it was made of silver, with some turquoise stones. He wore jeans and beautiful leather boots that looked like they were handmade.

Dr. Parker rushed over to the man as soon as he saw him. The two men walked towards the group together talking quietly, and then Dr. Parker introduced him.

"Everyone, this is John Bravebird," said Dr. Parker. "I met him when we were here last summer. He is a spiritual advisor from a local tribe who is going to lay a blessing here before we begin, which will hopefully allow our operation to go smoothly and safely."

They all stood quietly around John, as he said a few words in his tribe's language. Most of them had their eyes closed, but Jane kept one eye open as he spoke. She watched him take something that looked like tobacco out of a small pouch and sprinkle it on the ground in front of them.

"I have asked the spirits to understand and accept this operation, and to ask that no one will be hurt. This will help protect everyone," said John. "If you find that your equipment malfunctions and it seems everything is going wrong, then that is a sign that you need to stop what you are doing."

They all thanked John and Dr. Parker walked him back to his Jeep before he left.

The operation went fairly smoothly, but it took nearly all day to remove the gold bars and coins and haul them to the bank vault. Chris and Kendra and the girls helped however they could up on the mountain.

Jane and Peaches took a brief break sitting in the Jeep when they spotted a snake, but calmed themselves down fairly quickly and got back to work.

By the end of the day, everyone was exhausted. Jane, Peaches, Ashley and Edward rode back from the mountain to the house in Ashley's Jeep to shower and change. They saw Sarah in the kitchen, and sat at the table to talk to her.

"Jane, can you go ask Dr. Parker what time he thinks they'll be finished today?" asked Sarah.

"Sure," said Jane. She got up and went out to the front porch, just as Dr. Parker and Bubba and Rick had put the last load into the truck.

Suddenly, a dirty white pickup truck with New Mexico license plates pulled in and slammed on its brakes, creating a big cloud of dust that completely surrounded it. Three men jumped out. One was holding a gun and another man was holding binoculars.

Jane ducked down to hide behind the porch swing. She recognized the truck as the one that was in West Midland on her way home from the library.

"Stop right there," said the man that jumped out of the driver's side of the truck, pointing the gun at Dr. Parker. He motioned to Bubba and Rick. "Move over beside him." The two men that Dr. Parker had hired stood beside Dr. Parker.

The other two men from the white pickup tied up Dr. Parker, Bubba, and Rick to a nearby tree. They were sitting back-to-back-to-back and tied together around the trunk.

One of the men moved the white pickup next to the paneled truck. They had started moving the gold out of the paneled truck when Deputy Dave stepped out of his car, where he had been taking a coffee break. The other deputy, Luis, who had been standing by a tree watching all that happened, was poised with a rifle, waiting for the right moment to close in.

"Hands up! Drop your gun," said Deputy Dave. The three men looked surprised and stopped what they were doing.

"I said drop it," said Deputy Dave. The guy with the gun looked around and only then he saw the other deputy with a rifle aimed at him. He decided to drop his gun and raised his hands. The other two men finally set down the gold bars they were holding and raised their hands.

"Hands up against the truck," said Dave. The men complied and faced the side of the paneled truck with their hands on it.

Deputy Dave put handcuffs on all of them and then one by one, he put them all in the back of the police car, which had been parked behind Dr. Parker's truck and had not been visible to the intruders. Luis kept his rifle pointed at them during all of this. Once they were securely in the back of the police car, the deputies untied Dr. Parker, Rick and Bubba from the tree.

Deputy Luis drove the police car, while the paneled truck with Deputy Dave followed them into town to the bank. Another two deputies met the paneled truck at the bank. They helped with the unloading of the gold into the vault, while Dave and Luis took the bad guys to the local jail.

Jane was frozen in place behind the porch swing until after they left. She couldn't think of a way to help and was relieved that the deputies had everything under control. She couldn't believe what she had just witnessed. Her heart was beating wildly and she was so choked up she couldn't even swallow.

Sudden movement by the tree beyond the driveway caught Jane's eye. She thought she saw an American Indian with full headdress, nodding and smiling. He started to walk away and he disappeared into thin air. She rubbed her eyes and looked again but he wasn't there.

After watching the whole scenario, Jane went back into the house to report on what just happened. "It was the same pickup truck I saw in West Midland, and the guy with the gun was the one that I saw when I came out of the library. I followed him to that same truck. He's probably the one that pushed me in front of that car," said Jane.

"Goodness," said Sarah. "It seems like the deputies have things under control out there, though. It's a good thing they were here."

The girls and Edward stayed in the kitchen drinking lemonade, while Sarah had started working on dinner. Chris and Kendra rode back from the mountain in Andy's Jeep and came in next. They had no idea what happened until later, as they had been on their way back from the mountain when all the trouble occurred.

Andy was limping and had gauze tied around his calf. He had each arm around the shoulders of Chris and Kendra.

"What happened?" asked Sarah.

"Not a big deal," said Andy. "Just a snakebite. Kendra did a great job of handling it, and it wasn't a venomous snake."

"You're sure?" said Sarah, looking worried. "They can look similar."

"Oh, yeah. It was just a whipsnake," said Andy. "I know all the snakes in this area. I'm kind of an expert at this point."

"It still needs care, Andy," said Sarah.

"I agree. I had the first aid kit in the Jeep and Kendra had EMT training and handled everything. I've had snakebites before, so I don't go out there unless I'm prepared. She did everything that was needed."

"You took EMT training?" Sarah asked.

"Yes, ma'am. I've been volunteering with the

fire department ever since I finished high school. It seemed like having first aid skills of an Emergency Medical Technician is a good thing for an archaeologist, since we never know what kind of situation we might encounter on a dig," said Kendra.

"That's good thinking," said Sarah, nodding her head.

"I'm fine, don't worry," said Andy. "I'll call the doc if anything seems worrisome, and he'll come out. I need a shower." He limped to his room on his own.

Finally, Dr. Parker returned from the bank and Bubba and Rick left in the paneled truck.

Dr. Parker breathed a sigh of relief that the work was all over. He stopped by the kitchen and shared what happened with the rest of them and then went to his room to do some work on his computer.

CHAPTER EIGHTEEN

DINNER REVELATIONS

THE GIRLS STAYED in the kitchen to help Sarah prepare dinner. "Since it's your last night here, I thought we could all have a special dinner together," said Sarah. "Dr. Parker said he and the two students are leaving in the morning as well."

"That sounds fun," said Jane. "Thanks, Sarah. What else can we do to help?"

"I think I have everything under control now. Kaydee is preparing a few things, too. She and Dakota will join us for dinner. Kaydee promised to make some fry bread, in case you haven't tried it yet."

"I've heard of it," said Jane. "But I haven't tried it yet."

"It's a popular American Indian food. Everyone loves it and you will, too. Kaydee grew up on a reservation near here, so she knows how to cook some amazing American Indian dishes."

"Kaydee will join us for dinner?" asked Jane.

"Yes," said Sarah.

"I thought she might be worried about what might happen after taking the gold out of the cave," said Jane.

"Well, I'm sure she still is. And maybe the holdup outside was the bad thing and maybe it's all over now," Sarah replied.

"Oh yeah!" said Peaches. "Maybe that was the bad thing! Or maybe Andy's snake bite!"

"Maybe so. Since Dr. Parker was able to do it without disturbing any of the area around the cave, I think she'll feel a little better about it," said Sarah. "I didn't have any idea that she had seen any bones on the property at all. She's very quiet, and doesn't usually say much."

"Good, I'm glad she'll be there," said Jane. "I know that my friend Nate said that different cultures feel very strongly about what they believe."

"Yes, they do," said Sarah. "Dr. Parker is going to alert the authorities about the skeletons that you girls came across in the cave. In the case they are American Indians, they might want to re-bury them on their land. However, they might belong to the people who buried the gold, or maybe they are some treasure hunters that were here more recently."

"Yeah, I guess they could be anyone," agreed Ashley. "I'm glad they aren't us."

"Amen to that," said Peaches, nodding her head.

"How would they be able to tell the difference in a skeleton, whether it's an ancestor or a trespasser?"

asked Jane.

"I have no idea. The experts will have to figure that out," replied Sarah. "Anyway, for dinner tonight, we'll also have some Carne Adovada," she added.

"What's that?" asked Ashley.

"It's pork that is marinated ahead of time in a mixture of onion, red chile and other spices. I don't know anyone around here that doesn't like it, so I feel sure you girls will like it, too. We'll also have tacos, although they may be a little different from what you are accustomed to in the Midwest. Also, Andy will grill some green chile cheeseburgers."

"That sounds amazing!" said Peaches. "I'm hungry already!"

"I wanted to make sure you girls had a chance to taste some local favorites before you leave," said Sarah.

"You think of everything," said Peaches. "Maybe instead of a bed and breakfast, you should open a bed, breakfast and dinner."

Sarah laughed. "Maybe so."

"Were you able to get in touch with Jordan?" asked Jane.

"Yes, thank you for giving me his contact information. He was very helpful in answering some questions for me," said Sarah.

"Great," said Jane.

'I may have some news to share with all of you at dinner tonight," Sarah added.

"I can't wait!" said Peaches. "I hope it's something good."

"I hope so, too." Sarah smiled.

Later that evening, the entire group gathered on Sarah's patio in the backyard. Dakota and Kaydee were already there when the girls arrived, and Andy had the grill going with the green chile cheeseburgers. A long table was set up with an array of southwestern foods for everyone to share. Kaydee was setting the fry bread on the table when the girls arrived.

"This looks amazing!" said Peaches.

"And there are things I recognize, too," said Ashley. "Tacos and cheeseburgers! Yum!"

Edward had his nose in the air, sniffing the delicious aromas wafting in the air. "Sorry buddy, you already ate," said Ashley. "Mind your manners tonight." Edward looked up at her with his big moony eyes and tried to look invisible.

"That's a good boy," said Ashley, as she rubbed his neck.

Dr. Parker soon arrived on the patio with Chris and Kendra. "Everyone serve yourselves and have a seat at the table," Sarah announced, as soon as everyone was present.

Everyone started serving their plates and taking seats at the table. Jane noticed an empty chair at the end of the table. She thought she saw it scoot back and then move forward again by itself. She looked over and caught Sarah's eye as Sarah winked at Jane. When Jane sat down and looked again, a transparent outline of a person appeared in the evening light. Jane decided to ignore it and concentrate on her meal.

After everyone had a plateful of food and sat down, Sarah stood up. "I have an announcement to make." Everyone stopped talking and looked at Sarah with anticipation.

"After Jerome... er... Dr. Parker and I discussed the assessment of the gold that was discovered ... oh and also a big thank you to Ashley for falling into a literal gold mine while you were here..." Sarah nodded in Ashley's direction.

"You're welcome!" said Ashley with a big smile.

"And now that we have securely moved the gold to the bank vault and we've discussed it with a gold buyer, I have an idea of how much this treasure is worth. Quite a bit to be sure. This fortune is not worth much in its current form, so I will be cashing in the gold bars, since it was found on my land. I'm not sure what I'll do with the coins just yet."

Everyone nodded in agreement.

"The next step is to find a way to do something good with it. I've talked to Jordan Crowfoot from the Yellowglen Tribal Museum. I asked him for ideas on how best to use it to give back to the community that surrounds us."

Jane couldn't help thinking how much she admired Sarah for the way she thought about things.

Sarah continued. "We're going to start a smaller museum here in town to display whatever is found locally and that will include the items in my house that I've found on this land. I originally thought we would add to what is already in the museum that Jordan curates, but that is over 50 miles away. We'll have a smaller one here that is connected to the larger location, and Jordan will oversee the plans for it. Maybe we could call it the Chupacabra County Cultural Museum?"

Jane looked at Kaydee to see her reaction. Kaydee was listening intently, but showed no emotion.

"Also, Jordan expressed his desire for cultural traditions to be passed down through the generations, so some of the money will go to helping educate the children on their ancestral traditions, whatever that looks like. Jordan will have to explain that in more detail to me later."

Jane looked again at Kaydee. She was beginning to perk up and smile a bit.

"The last thing on my list so far, is to gift some money toward the Archaeology program at the West Midland University in Ohio, so that Dr. Parker's students can do more of their important work here in the future. I think that's a win-win for all of us."

"Of course, we will steer clear of any areas where there are buried ancestors, but they will do more excavations on my land near the house and we will display all of their finds in the new museum. Thanks everyone for your part in making all this happen so far and in the future."

Everyone clapped. Chris and Kendra smiled and gave each other a high five. Sarah started to sit down and then stood right back up.

"Oh, one more thing... Dakota and Kaydee, I am open to hearing your views on this. I want to do things the right way, but I think it's also important to do this to educate us on the history of our area and its people. Dr. Parker has a lot of knowledge in this area, and I trust him to handle any excavations carefully and with respect, but I also want to include you two and your views about what we discover. I'm really excited about this."

"Thank you," said Dakota. Kaydee nodded in agreement. "Kaydee was just trying to protect everyone when she put the sand paintings in the cave – just trying to warn you all against digging on the battlefield."

"What do you mean?" asked Sarah.

"I made sand paintings to warn you," said Kaydee.

"Why didn't you just tell me?" asked Sarah.

"That's not something we would do," said Dakota. "We don't want to encourage people to go digging where our ancestors are buried. We've heard the stories about Spanish treasure. All of a sudden this place could be ruined by people digging for treasure. We didn't know what you might do when you found out," said Dakota.

Kaydee finally explained. "I tried to warn you. I put the sand paintings inside the cave opening where Dr. Parker would find them to warn you all to stay away from the mountain."

Jane couldn't believe what she was hearing. All that research they had done couldn't have predicted that Kaydee was the one who created the sand paintings.

"You created the sand paintings?" asked Jane.

"Yes, when I found out the professor was coming to dig on this land, I put them in the cave where he would find them to warn him that this was sacred land – that our ancestors were buried here. Evil things can happen when you start digging on sacred land. You must never disturb the land where the warriors lay."

Jane looked at Dr. Parker. He looked totally surprised.

"I guess you didn't know you could trust us," said Dr. Parker gently. "But I didn't know when I looked at the paintings what the symbols meant. That would have taken a while to find out."

"I didn't know that," said Kaydee, looking down at her feet. "I thought you would know when you saw them and stay away."

"Well, luckily we were able to get the treasure out without disturbing the land. If Ashley hadn't fallen in the cave, we would have never gone up there," he said. "Any future excavations will remain near the house, where Sarah found evidence of a village. You can be involved as much as you wish with our projects."

Kaydee nodded.

Sarah lifted her glass and said, "It's been great having you all here and meeting you girls, and you too, Edward. It's going to seem very lonely after you all leave tomorrow. I hope you'll be able to come back soon. Now let's eat all this great food! Dig in!"

"Yeehaw!" said Peaches.

Dr. Parker was sitting across from Jane at the

table and noticed her necklace. "That's an interesting necklace, Jane," he said. "It looks like a coin."

"It was my mother's," Jane replied. "I haven't had it long, so I don't know anything about it."

"It looks similar to the ones that were found in the cave, although it is different," said Dr. Parker.

"I think you're right," said Jane. "Mine also has words engraved on the back of it."

"Oh," said Dr. Parker. "What does it say?"

"I don't know, actually. It's not in English."

"May I see it?" he asked.

"Sure," said Jane. She took off the necklace and handed it to Dr. Parker.

He read it out loud. "El viaje es la recompensa. That's Spanish."

"Do you know what it means?" asked Jane.

"Yes. It means 'the journey is the reward.' That's interesting. You said this was your mother's necklace?" said Dr. Parker. He handed it back to her.

"Yes. I don't know where she got it," said Jane. She put it back on. "Thank you. I've been wondering for months what it meant, but hadn't looked it up yet."

"Glad I could help," said Dr. Parker. "Have you found out anything about the coins in the cave yet?"

"So far, I found out that there are a number of different ways that the coins and gold could have gotten into the cave. Who only knows which treasure this could be?" said Jane.

"There are a lot of different stories that could point to this treasure," said Dr. Parker. "That's for sure."

"I found out that the Incas were mining gold back as far as 800 BC. Then Christopher Columbus sailed here from Spain looking for gold in the 1400s. He came here a few times, and then other people came here from Spain looking for gold, too."

"That's correct," said Dr. Parker. "Pizarro was one of them. He was a Spanish conquistador that went after gold from the Incas in Peru in the 1500s."

Jane continued. "I saw something mentioned about him. He held the emperor of the Incas hostage to get the Incas to bring him all their gold. It sounds like a lot of people were really gold crazy back then."

"There was a lot of craziness over it, yes," said Dr. Parker. "They needed wealth in some of the European countries and thought they could find it here and send it back to keep their economies going, which is what they did."

"I also read that there were also American Indian copper and turquoise mines in this area from hundreds of years before the Spanish had arrived here," said Jane. "The indigenous people used mined gold, silver, copper and other metals to create artistic and religious pieces. It sounds like they didn't care about making coins, though. So the gold coins make me think that all of these gold bars came from a place where the Spanish were making the coins, since it was all hidden together."

"Very good, Jane. That makes sense," said Dr. Parker. "They did make coins in South America and Mexico. Did you find where the mints were located?"

"Well, there were a lot of them," said Jane.

"Santo Domingo, Peru, Mexico City, Guatemala, Chile, and Columbia are some that I found. There are a bunch more, too. So the treasure could have come from a country in South America or Mexico, or maybe someone snatched it off one of those Spanish treasure fleets before it left."

"That is all good information, Jane," said Dr. Parker.

"There is also that guy that they think brought 16 tons of gold here from Mexico in his plane in the 1930s, and hid it somewhere in New Mexico," Jane added.

"I'm familiar with that story, and I don't think anyone has found it yet. He died without telling anyone where he hid it, so they say," said Dr. Parker.

"How much did we find?" asked Ashley.

"We don't know yet," said Dr. Parker. "When we get back to the Archaeology lab, we can research the coins further to find out where they were minted, and narrow down the options. We'll get some more good photos of them before we leave. This could keep us busy for a while, for there is a wealth of information about gold treasure and Spanish coins."

"When you said 'we', did you mean that I could be part of it?" said Jane.

"Only if you are interested," said Dr. Parker. "What you found was a good start on the research."

"Oh, yes. I would love to find out where this treasure came from, and who brought it here... if it's possible for us to know," said Jane.

"I think you'll learn a lot on your quest for the

answer. You might also discover something about the coin on your necklace," said Dr. Parker.

"I'm on board with that research, too," said Chris.

"Don't leave me out," said Kendra. "I'm totally in!"

"Fantastic," said Dr. Parker. "It should be an interesting semester. We still have all of the artifacts from our summer dig to process and research, plus the gold treasure. I can't wait until we are back at school and can get everyone started on this. We'll head out first thing in the morning."

CHAPTER NINETEEN

THE ARTIFACT

JANE WAS HAPPY to be back in her dorm room and back to her normal routine, although she had enjoyed the road trip and learning about new places. When Dr. Parker took students back to Sarah's dig site for the next excavation, Jane hoped she would be allowed to join them.

It seemed like they had been gone much longer than they actually were, because so much had happened. Jane did feel like her mission was accomplished after finding out the origin of the sand paintings, and was really surprised at the outcome. She hadn't seen Ashley for a week, since she'd been home and already missed her.

"Did your grandma send us any more of those brownies?" asked Peaches. "I was just thinkin' about how good they were."

"Yes, as a matter of fact, she did. It made her happy that we loved them so much," said Jane. She walked over to her dresser and pulled out the brownie container and handed it to Peaches. "Help yourself."

"Thanks!" said Peaches. She took two out of the container and set it on the dresser. "These are so good!"

'I know. They're my favorite," agreed Jane. "You're lucky I'm sharing them." Jane smiled and winked at her.

"Are you ready to go?" asked Peaches.

"Almost," said Jane. "I just need to put on my shoes. I'm so excited about this! Are you going to be part of the presentation?"

"I'm not sure exactly," said Peaches. "My dad just said to be at the West Midland Cultural Center at 1:00."

"Ready," said Jane, as she opened the door to their dorm room. Peaches headed out and Jane locked the door behind them. "I invited Nate to come. He's going to meet us there."

After a short walk, the girls reached the West Midland Cultural Center. There was a small group of people headed inside with them.

"I've never been in here before," said Jane, as she looked around the room. One room was entirely filled with display cases, and a second room also had some displays and a large table set up with chairs around it.

"I haven't either," Peaches whispered. "I wasn't sure what else was here. I think they just opened it a few years ago."

Jane spotted several rows of chairs at the end

of the second room facing a lectern with a microphone. Ashley and Nate were already sitting there waiting.

"There's Ashley and Nate," said Jane. "Let's go sit with them." They headed over and sat down beside them in the metal folding chairs.

"Hi stranger," said Nate, leaning in to whisper to Jane. "I missed you."

"And I missed you. I wish you could've gone with us," said Jane.

"Me, too," said Nate. "I can't believe what you girls found. I'm totally amazed."

"I can't believe it either," said Jane.

"So are we on for Friday night dinner this week? Just the two of us?" Nate whispered. "You can catch me up on the details."

"Sounds good," said Jane. "I'm looking forward to it." She felt her heart skip a beat.

Peaches looked up and saw Carl come in the door. "Carl!" she whispered loudly to get his attention and waved him over.

Carl sat down beside Peaches. "So good to see you up and around," said Peaches.

"How are you?" said Jane, leaning over to talk around Peaches, who was sitting between them. She noted that he still looked like he was recovering from his injury.

"I'm much better," said Carl. He winced as he touched his hand to his forehead. "I really am. Thanks."

The head of the center, Madeline Krumpet,

walked up to the microphone and asked everyone to sit down for the presentation. "I would like to introduce Dr. Jerome Parker, Professor of Archaeology at our own West Midland University. Dr. Parker is here to present a new artifact for our center," said Madeline.

"Thank you, Madeline, and thank you all for coming," said Dr. Parker, as he stood up and shook her hand.

"If you haven't been to the center before, I urge you to spend some time looking around at all of the artifacts that have been found right here in West Midland. It is believed that a native village with around 400-500 people was located here in the 1600s."

"If you are here for the presentation, you likely already know about the serpent mound that runs along the bluff on River Street. It was quite a fascinating discovery decades ago, and several rounds of excavating were completed a while back. Currently there is no digging going on at all. It's been covered with a thick layer of dirt and preserved as green space with park access."

He then pulled out the artifact that Peaches had found and set it on the lectern in front of him, covered by a cloth.

"We haven't had any new artifacts for a while, since there are no excavations going on, so it was a surprise to me when my daughter, Peaches, found something exciting. She wasn't digging, of course, but discovered this artifact sticking out of the side of the bluff while hiking on the trail. Please stand up,

Peaches."

Peaches stood up and everyone applauded. "My friend, Jane, was with me when we made the discovery," she said. Peaches pulled Jane by the arm to stand up with her. Everyone applauded for Jane. The girls sat back down.

"And here it is," said Dr. Parker, as he uncovered the artifact and held it up. "It's a beaded coup stick in very good condition. The eagle feathers are a little worn from being in the ground, but after cleaning it up a bit, it looks well preserved overall."

The audience oohed and aahed and then clapped again.

Dr. Parker continued explaining. "When the men in the village went to war, they used the coup stick to show bravery by touching the enemy with it without killing him. Often the brave warrior would receive an eagle feather for doing this and he would attach it to his coup stick. This makes me believe that this was a peaceful village, not full of warmongers, but they did what was needed to stand their ground and show a force of strength when enemies were encountered."

"I wondered what that was used for," whispered Jane. "It really is a cool find."

"Yeah, cool," whispered Peaches.

"We are going to place the item in this display case over here," said Dr. Parker, as he walked over to the case and set it in there. I encourage you all to come take a look at it before you leave. Thank you all for coming!"

Everyone clapped and then got up and started

THE MYSTERY ON SNAKE MOUNTAIN, A Jane Teaberry Mystery

milling around to look at all the displays.

"That was pretty cool," said Ashley. "I'm glad you girls didn't get in any trouble for digging it up."

"We didn't dig it up," said Jane.

"It was sticking almost all the way out of the bluff," said Peaches. "It would have just fallen into the river."

"Okay, okay, I'm sorry. I didn't know you girls were so sensitive about it." Ashley laughed.

"See you girls later," said Carl. He walked over to look at the displays.

"I need to talk to your dad for a minute," said Jane to Peaches.

"Um, okay," said Peaches. She and Ashley started looking around at the displays.

Jane waited until Dr. Parker was finished with a conversation, and then stepped over to talk to him.

"Hi Dr. Parker," said Jane.

"Hello Jane," said Dr. Parker. "It's a wonderful artifact," he said with a smile. "A great addition to the center."

"I've never seen one of those before," said Jane. "I didn't know what it was. Um, I just wanted to tell you that I've decided to major in Archaeology. I really find all this stuff fascinating and want to be part of the program. I just wanted to let you know that," said Jane.

"Well, that's wonderful news," said Dr. Parker. "I guess I'll be seeing more of you in the lab."

"I guess you will," said Jane with a smile.

"By the way, I heard from Deputy Dave this

morning," Dr. Parker continued. "The men in the pickup truck that tried to rob us confessed that they had overheard Kaydee in the antique shop when she asked about the Spanish coins. They were spying on the Emmons estate trying to figure out where she found them, and then saw us arrive during the summer and spied on our dig. They've been staying near Sarah's house in an old ghost town."

"The Lost Horses?" asked Jane.

"The what?" asked Dr. Parker, looking confused.

"I mean, Los Caballos Perdidos. Is that where they were staying?" asked Jane.

"I don't know where exactly. I just know that it was nearby so they could watch what we were doing," said Dr. Parker. "They had followed our student group back to Ohio, thinking we may have found some of the treasure. They thought the sand paintings might be a map to the treasure, and they are the ones that broke in and attacked Carl. So that solves that mystery."

"Wow," said Jane. "I'm glad they're locked up. Carl must be so relieved."

"I imagine so," nodded Dr. Parker. "I know I am. I want the lab to be a safe place for students. Jane, we wouldn't know any of this if you hadn't taken the initiative to look into those stolen paintings. Thank you for everything you did to investigate the burglary at the lab. I'm not sure if the police would have been able to figure this one out."

Jane smiled. "I'm glad I could help, Dr. Parker."

"Excuse me, I have to talk to these people over

here," said Dr. Parker. "Welcome to the program, Jane."

Jane started looking around at the displays. Nate walked over to her when he was finished looking at everything. "I have to get back to work," he said.

"Oh, that's too bad," said Jane. "I'm glad you could come."

"I'll see you Friday, or even sooner if you wanna stop by the library," said Nate.

"I might if I have time," said Jane.

When the girls were all finished looking around, they met at the door. "Are you ready for our picnic?" she asked.

"Yeppers," said Ashley. "Edward is waiting in the Jeep."

"We're walking," said Jane. "I'll grab our order from the Village Café and we'll meet you and Edward at the shelter at the serpent head – you know, down by the cemetery from the old village."

"Don't remind me that it's a cemetery. It's a park now," said Ashley.

"Okay, meet you at the park then." Jane laughed.

"That's better," said Ashley.

As they ate their lunch at the park shelter, Jane told Ashley and Peaches of her decision to major in Archaeology.

"I'm sure you'll enjoy it," said Peaches. "I can see that already."

"Great decision, cousin," said Ashley, nodding in agreement.

"Did your dad find out anything about that rolled-up sheepskin in the bottle that Ashley found in the cave?" asked Jane. "You know, like what the writing on it said?"

"Not yet," said Peaches. "But maybe it'll tell us where the rest of the treasure is buried."

"The rest of the treasure?" Ashley laughed.

"What else would it be?" asked Peaches.

"No idea," said Ashley. "Maybe it is more treasure, or maybe it's the directions to the one we found."

"Why would they write directions to a place and then leave them in that place?" asked Jane. "That doesn't make sense."

"I don't know," said Ashley. "I guess we'll have to wait until Dr. Parker figures out what it says. "

Just then, Jane started to hear the faint sound of tribal drumbeats again. "Listen. Do you hear it now?" said Jane.

"What?" said Ashley.

"I don't hear anything," said Peaches.

"The drumbeats, the singing," said Jane, getting frustrated. "Tell me that you hear it, too."

"Don't worry, Jane, I believe you, even if I can't hear it. After the singers in The Lost Horses church, I'll believe anything," said Peaches.

"Same here," said Ashley. "No one saw Chief Goodfeather except for me, and I guess, Sarah, when she was a kid."

"I think I may have seen him," said Jane. "He was watching from beside a tree when those guys were arrested in Sarah's front yard."

"Really?" said Peaches. "How cool! Maybe he is always around, like Sarah said."

Edward stood up suddenly and looked toward the trees wagging his tail and jumping around with excitement.

"Aha," said Jane. "At least Edward can hear them. I guess it's just you and me this time, Edward."

***

Review Request

Thank you for taking the time to read this book. I hope you enjoyed it and found the story to be entertaining.

I would love to have your feedback, and would be grateful if you would post an honest review of the book. Your feedback does make a difference.

1. To leave a review, please visit *The Mystery on Snake Mountain* book page on Amazon.com.
2. Scroll down to the *Customer Reviews* section.
3. Locate the button labeled *Write a customer review* and click the button to enter your review.

Thank you in advance for your feedback! Look for Jane's first adventure, *The Secret Behind the Bookcase*, on Amazon.com or check your local bookstore.

For further information, please contact the author at info@hundredacrepress.com.

Or snail mail to:
Hundred Acre Press LLC
P.O. Box 54316
Cincinnati, OH 45254

Made in the USA
Monee, IL
07 November 2023